MONSTER IN THE MIST

MONSTER IN THE MIST

CALDER GARRET

for my painted forebears

CONTENTS

WE FOLLOW THE LOCH

Our habits are poorly woven and give us just the barest protection from the bitter wind that blows across the loch, and the soles of our sandals are but paper thin and offer us even less assurance against the slippery mosses and lichens that grow beneath our feet. At any moment, any one of us might slip and fall, or an evil gust might tear us from the others and deliver us unto the water. And from the murky depths of the loch, we have been told, there is no return.

There are thirteen of us gathered here on the bank of this loch, each of us following in the footsteps of the one before, walking in deepest silence, in deepest contemplation. Twelve of us are novices; some, like Brother Eamon, are just eighteen summers old, while others, like myself, are an older and wiser twenty-two. Each of our number has, in his own way and for his own reasons, chosen to follow our beloved shepherd, Father Melachlin, one time Abbot of Killeaney, the wisest of us all. We are all of us, in some sense, delicate creatures in an indelicate realm. We are all creatures of God in a fallen world.

Father Melachlin moves slowly, so slowly I can see the youngest of our brethren growing frustrated. They wish for a faster pace and would clearly prefer to be walking upon the safer, more solid ground only a few steps away. But any prayers they might make to this aim are fruitless. It is as if our dear Father Melachlin has a lesson to teach. But even to me, and I rank myself amongst the most astute of our group, his message is a mystery.

Nearly four days have passed since our arrival into this cursed country and in this time we have walked with little rest. We have not gone thirsty – the loch has provided us with all the fresh water needed to fill our bellies – but we have eaten only what we have been able to forage – some wild grasses, berries and roots and the occasional small fish we have scooped from the loch. Little by little, piece by piece, each of us has become a tired and hollow shell.

And the weather here, we have quickly found, is as hellish as the land itself. Day and night, it offers us no pity. While the summer sun rises daily to scorch and test us, its nightly absence, if it were possible, brings us even more distress. Father Melachlin has forbidden us even the warmth of a fire, so when evening falls, each of us feels the Devil's icy fingers digging deep into our flesh. But it is best, the Father insists, that we do not draw attention to ourselves. It is best, he says, that we shun the native people until our time to proselytise has come.

As hard as it has been, we have come to understand and accept our leader's decision. Even we, as novices, have, from the evidence we have acquired, come to accept that all precautions need to be taken. Monks who have been here before have shared with us the most incredible tales of danger and intrigue. And even from our small understanding of those apparently more civilised people living closer to the coast, we can tell. This is a far fiercer and more brutal place than our native Hibernia could ever be.

Nearly eight hundred years have passed since the death of our Saviour, and His Good News has now reached most of the known world. It has reached the farthest shores of our beloved homeland and spread throughout the Anglo-Saxon south of this island. But even so, there are still many places where our Lord is hard to find. The dark and frozen north, it is told, remains a home to the most pagan of customs. And while here in this nameless place there are now pockets of what we might call faith and civilisation, for the most part the people, if we can indeed call them people, remain Godless heathens. It is the mission of our happy brethren to minister to these souls, to bring them, these so-called 'painted' folk, these 'Picti', into the body of Christ.

There are few sounds to hear, just the wind over the water, the lapping of the waves and the occasional singing of the birds in the bushes nearby. I cannot tell what they are singing about. There is nothing around us that brings any form of pleasure. My only joy, and even this is forbidden, is the odd whisper from Brother Eamon behind me. We exchange amusements, jokes if you like, mostly about the terribly round frame of Brother Aengus waddling before us and the dirty marks on the rear of Brother Conall's habit. We are poor examples, I have decided, of either brotherhood or the spirit of Christ.

But for Eamon, I have had little to do with any of my brothers. The conditions on the ship from Hibernia gave us no room for conversation and since our landing, Father Melachlin has imposed upon us this strict vow of silence. Only the most necessary communication is permitted, during emergencies or in the preparation of meals. Even in the meals' consumption, we have been told to hold our tongues.

We are, in a sense, shackled and must, at all times, obey the will of Father Melachlin by remaining reflective and still. But even in this quietude, I can tell. Brother Eamon is the spriteliest, most good-natured of lads. And I can also attest. With his soft blond hair and sparkling blue eyes, he is the most handsome of us. His smile, if we ever were in one again, would light up a room. I could make jokes about the teeth of my other brothers, but they are perhaps best saved for another day.

Most of us come from the rabble, being the third or fourth sons of craftsmen or, at best, minor chieftains. But Brother Eamon, he happily tells me, is the second son of a second son in the family Ui Briuin. He is the grandson of a king. Why then, I ask him, did he choose the clergy? Why did he choose to follow Father Melachlin to this lost land? Or was the path chosen for him, I ask. No, he replies. Even from an early age, he knew. His was the path of knowledge and learning. His was the path of faith.

WE MEET THE PICTS

Before us we discover a small but welcome stretch of sand and then another rocky outcrop which we must scale before we can see what lies beyond. But even before we reach the rocks, we hear a change in the air. We hear human voices, but not the kind of quiet conversation. These voices are loud, some fearful, some angry, all in a language we cannot understand.

Most of us huddle in fear, keen to retrace our steps back along the shoreline. Even I, and I consider myself brave as well as canny, look to Father Melachlin, hoping for some comforting words. But the good Father merely sinks to one knee and, signalling for us to do the same, hushes us even more.

'Brother Aengus,' he whispers, drawing his finger to his lips. 'Quiet your heart. I can hear its beating even here.'

He looks to Brother Feargus, the only one of us to have travelled this land before, and draws him closer.

'Feargus, my son,' he says. 'Pray tell me. Of what do they speak?'

Feargus listens. The rest of us remain still, awaiting his interpretation.

'There has been a death, dear Father,' says Feargus, finally. 'A terrible death. The death of the tribe's most famous warrior. They have found his body ... his headless body ... floating in the waters of the loch.'

We gasp collectively and Father Melachlin glares, with the anger of Elijah.

'And why do they argue, Brother?' he asks.

Feargus hesitates, as though worried his answer might bring the Father's disapproval.

'Some are saying ...' he answers slowly. 'Some are saying the death is a punishment by their gods for the man's arrogance and pride.'

'And the others?' asks Father Melachlin.

'Most ...' says Brother Feargus. 'Most believe he was the victim of a beast. A mighty beast that hides in the depths of the loch. This beast has been known, on nights when the moon is full, to rise up and claim any who wander too close to the water.'

Each of us shuffles away from the shore and onto the dry sand. But Father Melachlin begins to climb the rocks.

'Come, my children,' he says. 'This may be the sign we have waited for. This may be the time for us to share our Lord's Good News.'

We follow, but with little enthusiasm. Without saying so, we agree. We will be lucky to survive this encounter. Even our arrival in the west was met with a barrage of rotten cabbage, turnips and stinking sheep shit.

We lift ourselves over the rocks and, gaining a vantage just before the peak, we peer over. What we see is just as our ears might have described. Within a ring of the most rudimentary stone huts stands a group of natives. There are perhaps fifty of them, all half-naked, with their bodies and faces, men and women alike, marked with the most intricate of designs. Stars, swirls and crescent moons, in all shade of blue, adorn their skin. And their heightened debate is in a language most fit for swine. As one, we wait for Father Melachlin to act.

By way of summers on God's green Earth, our dear Father Melachlin is not so old. At most, he is perhaps in his sixtieth year. But it seems he has done everything in his power to look older and, as a result, wiser. His hair and beard are long and ragged, and have long since turned the whitest of whites. His habit comes in a faded grey rather than the muddy brown we novices wear. And only at the rarest of times do his staff and his rosary leave his hands.

God, the Father tells us, will protect us. It is He and He alone who will guide us and keep us. In Christ's hands, we have nothing to fear, the Father says, from either Satan or from the heathens and their satanic ways. With these words delivered and with his lips pressed hard against his rosary, he leads us down from the rocks and towards the huddled throng below.

It takes them a moment to notice us, too busy are they with their arguing, but, one by one, the Picts stop and, turning, take us in. I feel Brother Eamon's hand reaching for mine. It is such an odd and unexpected feeling, my immediate reaction is to pull away. But then I realise. The boy is younger and much more fearful than the rest of us. So I take his hand and squeeze, offering as much reassurance as I can.

'Do you think ...?' he whispers. 'Are we safe?'

Already, we can see the swords, knives and axes at the sides of these unGodly beasts.

'We can only hope,' I reply. 'And pray.'

Father Melachlin leads us to within a dozen steps of the now murmuring crowd and then, like Moses towards the waters of the Red Sea, he waves his staff and gestures. To our astonishment and, I think, out of their own surprise, the Picts obey. Like the Sea, they part, revealing the object of their gaze. It is, truly enough and as Brother Feargus has described, a body. It is muscular, mighty and almost totally blue, not yet from death, but from the strange patterns with which these people deface their bodies. And, as Brother Feargus has said, its head is nowhere to be seen. As if by a mighty axe, the head has been hewn from the body and taken either to a Pictish netherworld or into the freezing depths of the loch.

THE WOMAN

I can feel the eyes of the crowd upon us, as if they may be deciding our fate. I can sense their deep suspicion and, I think, their readiness to send us quickly into the arms of our Lord. But Father Melachlin shows no fear.

'Feargus,' he says. 'Have them tell us of the fate of this poor wretch.'

Feargus begins to stutter, as though suspecting that in speaking their tongue, he might somehow draw the natives' ire. But they listen, their eyes falling on Father Melachlin, who they now recognise as our leader. After a moment, Feargus grows quiet and the Picts begin to argue. But then, from the back of the crowd, some sharp words are heard and they hush. A woman steps forward, drawing her sword as she comes. Father Melachlin spreads his arms, as if to protect us.

Apart from the occasional piece of well-placed cloth, a few ornaments and what appears to be a bear skin wrapped around her shoulders, this woman is nearly naked. So much so that we brothers must avert our eyes. At least we try. Despite the primitive markings on her face and limbs, and even with her flashing blade, only the most devout of us would find her unappealing. She is tall, well-toned, and her long black hair hangs about her waist.

The Picts, I have heard, count women as well as men among their chieftains. Until now, I had considered this a falsehood. But it is obvious that this woman carries weight within her tribe. Her dark eyes challenge us, fixing time after time on each of us brothers. Her gaze is strong and I know that, in my own body at least, it stirs a deep uneasiness. Finally, she looks deep into the eyes of our Father Melachlin and speaks.

'She wishes to know who we are, Father,' says Feargus. 'Are we perchance angels sent by the gods or are we instead demons, in league with the monster in the loch?'

We look to each other. Our ragged, filthy attire, we think, points towards the latter. But Father Melachlin, of course, remains strong.

'Tell her we are neither,' he says. 'Neither. But tell her, if she will listen, that we bring news. The Good News of our own God, the one true God.'

Feargus forces the words and we await the woman's reply. After a moment, there is laughter within the crowd and Feargus takes a step backwards into our group.

'She says she has heard stories,' Feargus says, 'of

men from the west claiming to be men of peace. Men who carry no weapons and leave their fate to God.'

Our chests puff with pride for a moment, happy with such labels.

'But she says these men are fools,' Feargus continues. 'If we are such men, she says, our God will not protect us, neither from the point of her sword nor, worse still, from the teeth of the monster in the loch.'

We feel our peril and each seeks shelter one behind the other. But Father Melachlin continues on, undaunted.

'Tell her I agree,' he says. 'Tell her she is correct. If she, or any one of her people, were to use their swords against us, there is nothing any of us could do but meet our maker with faith and hope in our hearts. Faith and hope that our path into His glory is secure. But tell her also. Tell her that our hearts would also be filled with love for those that send us there.'

These words, uttered by Brother Feargus with as much confidence as he can muster, seem to confuse the Godless brutes. It seems, I think, that any softer notions such as mercy and gentility are quite unknown to them.

'But add, Brother Feargus,' the Father says, now raising both his staff and his voice. His face turns the deepest red. 'Tell them that our God is a vengeful God. Were they to harm any one of us, he would deliver unto them the most terrible retribution.'

The Picts fall silent. It is as if our dear Father has either broken through to them or, in his fury, sealed our fate. All eyes fall on the woman as she considers. Then, in one swift graceful motion, she returns her sword to its scabbard.

Father Melachlin breathes a deep breath. He, too, thinks to himself, before turning to us, his followers.

'We can relax, now, Brothers, I believe,' he says. 'It appears there is no more cause for alarm.'

But I cannot help but notice the ashen faces of my brethren. It seems as if these words have done little to calm their trembling hearts. We remain huddled together, like a flock of Cruachan caera.

'Can we be certain of this, Father?' I say.

I am surprised by the tremor in my own voice.

'Yes. And there is more, Brother Niall,' the Father says. 'For now, I believe, is a time for us to take heart. The Lord, in his wisdom, has spoken to me. This, He has said, is the opportunity to proselytise we have been waiting for.'

'How might this be, Father?' I find myself asking.

The Father speaks to us all in a low, tranquil tone.

'Listen to me, my children,' he says. 'The Lord has revealed to me how we might use this situation to our advantage. He has told me that we must seize this moment and call upon His strength to banish the beast from these waters. Then, these Picts will become full of gratitude. They will become eager and willing to accept all the love and grace the Almighty offers.'

'But really, Father?' I ask. 'Can we actually do this? Will the Lord really help us drive the creature away?'

'All things are possible, my son,' says Father Melachlin. He smiles and places a comforting hand on my shoulder. 'All things are possible with a modicum of faith.'

With these words on his lips, the Father steps forward. In all confidence, he leads us even closer to the crowd and towards the body. And like that flock of sheep, we fall in behind him.

THE WARRIOR'S BODY

Yes, like sheep we shuffle forward, with those of us with any strength at all seeking security behind the weak, pushing these poor unfortunates, Brother Eamon amongst them, towards the fangs of the hungry wolves. But we need not worry. A truce, it seems, has indeed been established between Father Melachlin and the woman. For now, at least, we are safe and able to relax.

Approaching the body and prodding it lightly with his staff, Father Melachlin speaks to the woman again.

'This man?' he says. 'Ask her, please, Brother Feargus. Was he a man of importance in the tribe?'

Feargus waits for the woman's response. He replies in time.

'He was a chieftain, of sorts,' he says. 'He was her husband ... but also her brother.'

We all look to Father Melachlin, astonished, gauging his response, but he remains stone-faced.

'And the beast in the loch?' he asks. 'If such a thing exists. Please. Bid her tell us more. How frequently does it come?'

'More and more frequently in the past few months,' says Brother Feargus. 'She says that in the past few years, every spring and summer, it has come to claim its prey.'

I sense an uneasiness amongst some of my brothers. We have been on our feet since early morning and, both troubled and tired, most of them now desire an escape from this knotted conversation. The good Father, I can tell, notices it, too. So, for the first time in many days, he frees us from our bondage. At least, most of us.

'Brothers,' he says. 'I can tell that you need rest. Go. You are free to mingle amongst the people here, to communicate with them if you can, and, providing you do not lay with their women, befriend them. Brother Feargus ... and Brother Niall, I ask that you attend me while I explain my desire to ... Feargus, ask this woman. What is her name?'

The woman replies with little more than a grunt.

'Domelch,' says Feargus. 'Her name is Domelch,'.

'And is she now chief of the tribe?' asks Father Melachlin. 'Now that her brother ... her husband ... is dead?'

'She says she was and remains a chieftain, too,' says Feargus. 'She was superior to the man even before his death. And more so now.'

My thoughts about this profane matrilineal practice are true.

'Domelch,' asks Father Melachlin. 'When will you send your brother ... to the gods? On his journey to the afterworld?'

Feargus and I catch each other's eye. We are not used to hearing the Father speak such nonsense. But Feargus interprets for him.

'In the morning,' comes the reply. 'When the sun rises.'

'In which case,' says Father Melachlin. 'Ask her, Feargus. If she and her people will permit, we shall call upon our Lord immediately afterwards to free them from this demon that plagues them. Tell her we will draw upon His strength to do the incredible and rid the loch of this terrible creature forever.'

The woman laughs and, for the first time, makes physical contact with one of us. She shakes the old man vigorously and, grabbing his nether parts, laughs some more.

'She says if we have the courage, Father, we are welcome to try,' says Feargus. 'But she doubts that where she and her tribe have failed with arrows and spears, we will succeed with merely words and hot air.'

'Tell her we will succeed, Feargus,' says the Father. 'Tell her we have enduring faith in our Lord. But tell her also. Tell her when we do succeed, we expect her and her people to accept His strength and His power.'

'And, Father?' I intrude. 'Should we not also ...? Rather than accept a pagan rite, should we not also offer them a Christian burial for this man? It may show them we mean well.'

'No, Brother Niall,' says the Father. 'It may tell them just the opposite. I believe that many of these people choose to burn their dead. If we were to bury him with foreign words, they may think we were sending him to Hell ... No. For now, we must tolerate their practices and fit in with their society as best we can.'

I notice as several women approach and, lifting the body, carry it away.

'Where are they taking him?' I ask.

The woman seems surprised I have spoken directly to her, but when Feargus interprets, she answers kindly.

'He must be prepared for his journey,' says Feargus. 'Even though his head ... his mind and soul ... has been taken, he must be given all the honour he deserves. He will be washed and cleaned and painted anew.'

'May I ...?' I turn to Father Melachlin. 'Father, will you permit me, if it is indeed allowed ... Will you permit me to follow and watch this ritual?'

Father Melachlin seems a little puzzled, but also content to accept my curiosity. Brother Feargus submits my request to the woman.

'She says you are welcome to watch,' says Feargus. 'But in silence. You must not speak or interrupt the work. But first ...'

Brother Feargus breaks into a grin, which I know is a good sign.

'But first,' he says. 'She asks us ... Their evening meal has been prepared and there is plenty. She invites us to join them.'

I pray that Father Melachlin will allow us to break what seems like a never-ending fast.

'Thank her,' says the Father. 'Tell her if she will permit me to pray over the meal, we will be happy to join them.'

The woman laughs again.

'So long as you do not shit in the pot,' says Brother Feargus, 'she says you can do whatever you like.'

THE POT BOILS

I ask the good Father for permission to leave and, seeing Brother Eamon among others huddled around an open fire in the clearing between the huts, I join them. Several Picts are also gathered and a hefty, tattooed brute stirs a large cauldron. It feels good to embrace the warmth. It is the first time I have seen a fire in days, and the aroma from the pot, whatever is cooking, attends every fibre of my being. Although I accept I will be misunderstood, I exchange a few words with the cook.

'What,' I ask, 'is cooking there?'

The cook replies with a quizzed look and I try communicating with some signs. I point to the pot and then to my mouth, before replicating, as best I can, the actions and noises of some common beasts – a sheep, a cow, a deer. But the Pict looks perplexed. He utters something to his companions and they burst into laughter. He bellows back at me and reaches down to his waist. Then, for the first time, I notice hanging there, a collection of heads. There are three or more, each attached to his belt by what little hair remains on it. At first glance, I imagine they are those of large animals, perhaps bears or wolves, and represent hunting trophies of some sort. But at a second look, I realise. To my horror, they are human, in some way withered and shrunken and each in an advanced state of decay.

'Dear God,' I gasp, stepping back. 'Surely not ...?'

Then the brute makes a cutting motion across his throat and makes to drop his own head into the pot. I look to my brothers. It is as if they, like myself, are turning as blue as the natives.

'What shall we tell Father Melachlin?' says Eamon. 'Surely none of us can eat this devil's stew.'

'We shall say nothing yet, Eamon,' I say. 'In fact, I am yet to be convinced that this man is doing anything but trying to frighten us. Watch and learn.'

I signal to the man for a bowl and, digging deep, I fill a ladle. As far as I can see, based on this meal at least, the Picts are solely carnivores. There seem to be no vegetables in the stew at all, only large pieces of white, fatty meat. But truthfully, even if the meat were human, I have been so long without, I would still be sorely tempted.

My fingers burn as I reach into the bowl, but, retrieving a large piece of meat, I push it deep between my teeth. Then, with all eyes, the Picts' and those of my brothers, watching me, I chew. My brethren cross themselves and whisper in disbelief. The Pict and his fellows grin. Nevertheless, despite every desire to the contrary, I continue to chew. Finally, I am able to swallow the cursed meat. I make a show of it, offering my tongue and casting the remains of my bowl back into the pot.

'Was that not a sin, Brother?' says Eamon. 'Is it not against God's law to eat the flesh of man?'

'It is indeed, Eamon,' I say. 'But I have a sense that was no more human flesh than it was that of a lion.'

I make the strongest eye contact with the cook.

'Tell me truly, now,' I say. 'What animal was it? Was it a boar? A pig?'

I fork my imaginary tail and flatten my nose, offering several porcine squeals. The Picts among us cheer and offer similar actions in return.

'How did you know, Brother Niall?' asks Eamon.

'The truth is I did not,' I say. 'I still do not. My only thought is that it is better for these people to think us fools than to think us cowards.'

Father Melachlin, Feargus and the woman approach and the Father says his words over the pot. Then, while the Picts laugh and carouse over their meal, my brethren and I eat ravenously, but quietly. It is as if the habit of silence has become ingrained in us.

As I watch him devour spoonful after spoonful of his meal, I decide it is better not to share my doubts and concerns about the contents of the pot with Father Melachlin. Whatever the truth, my brethren and I are starving and if we are to enjoy the full meal we so desperately need, it is better, I decide, that the good Father believes that it is indeed a pig boiling away there in the broth. The notion that we may be devouring the flesh of some man who has wronged this tribe is something I will keep to myself. It is on my own soul that we may be becoming as bad as the heathens.

THE BODY IS PREPARED

T he noises and smells emitted by the heathens post-meal are enough to drive us from the fire. Father Melachlin takes us away for some prayer. And as I listen to him mutter, I cannot help but wonder. How does he expect us to deliver the Picts from the beast? Can we really succeed, I wonder. Or am I just showing my own lack of faith? Yes, perhaps I am. I must be.

The truth of it, I have decided, can only be that Father Melachlin places no great store in the existence of the monster. The very notion of a terrible beast living in the loch, he must believe, is naught but superstition. For, all faith aside, if he truly gave credence to its dangers, I doubt he would have made his offer so quickly. If this is so, then we must rely in his judgement. And our task of banishing the thing will be an easy one. But I cannot help but worry. What will the Picts' reactions be if the monster is, in fact, real and our efforts fail? Whatever the case, I tell myself, the morning, when it arrives, will define the future for our little crew.

Our prayers finished, I watch as the same handful of women carry torches into the largest of the huts. This, I know, is the temporary resting place of the warrior's body. It is, I assume, where they will wash and prepare it for tomorrow's pyre. I receive the Father's permission again and, making my excuses to my brothers, I follow the women. I am keen to see the complete ritual, not just the final moments.

The inside of the hut is spacious enough and, with four torches burning, well lit. But it is smoky and the air is pungent, not from the body's decay but from some form of incense the women have chosen to burn. The body, now naked, is laid out on a tablet in the middle of the hut and the four women surrounding it have begun a low and mournful chant. Is it in their language or gibberish? I have no idea. It is enough to say it is meaningless to me. I notice a stool on the perimeter of the space. Thankful the women have shown no interest in my presence, I move it close to the doorway, in the hope I might breath some fresh air, and sit.

The women begin with the sharpest blades I have ever seen. I fear they are about to cut the poor man, disembowel him or worse. But my fears are unwarranted. They are shaving him, scraping his skin from top to toe, front and back. And yes, to my embarrassment, they shave his nether parts too. They shave him until not a hair remains. I wonder, had his head been still attached, would they have shaved that too?

This is my first opportunity to view the body up close. The man must indeed have been, I decide, a mighty warrior. Even headless, I surmise he would be taller than any amongst our group. He has the muscles of someone who has chosen to live with an enormous amount of strenuous activity. And all parts of his skin are marked with tattoos of the deepest blue.

But as I look at the great absence that was his head, I cannot help but wonder. There is no uneven mark, such as one might expect from a tooth, of whatever size. The cut is clean, done in one strike, such as with an axe or with a sword. Is there subterfuge at play here, I wonder. In blaming the monster in the loch, have the heathens hidden the real wrongdoer from us? Has Father Melachlin, without realising, brought us into an even deeper mystery than we might have imagined?

The chanting continues as one of the women reaches for a small receptacle and places it on the tablet next to the body. Each of the women reaches in and grabs a handful of … To begin with, I am not sure what it is. It is white and soft … It is only when they begin rubbing the substance into the body that I realise. It is fat, perhaps the excess fat from the animal we have just eaten. And its purpose? I make a simple and confident deduction. It is to help the body burn when they put it to the torch.

The chanting goes on long into the night, becoming, for me, an endless drone. It has been a long day and with a full belly and what passes for a comfortable chair, I find it easy to close my eyes. The hut is warm enough and even if I snore, the women will give me no mind.

But when I awaken, the hut is dark and cold. The women have gone and have taken the body with them. I rub my eyes and shake myself awake and, leaving the hut, head for the nearby brush to relieve myself.

I CONVERSE WITH THE FATHER

I t is still dark, but the morning star is shining brightly and I can see activity by the shore of the loch. Preparations are being made to the funeral pyre, a torch to be added in time with the first rays of the sun. I look around for my brothers, at first near the pyre and then the huts. A small fire burns at some distance from the huts and I see Father Melachlin seated on a log warming his hands. The good Father, I realise, seems to survive with very little sleep. My brethren, on the other hand, are quite indolent. With their arses to the fire, they lay grunting and coughing and farting and digging themselves into the dirt like the heathens' drove of swine.

I join them and, not wanting to disturb their sleep, I sit on the log beside Father Melachlin. Two pots rest on the fire nearby. Father Melachlin drinks from a cup that smells of apples and an empty bowl lies at his feet. He drains the cup and offers both cup and bowl to me.

'They have provided us with breakfast,' he says. 'A porridge of sorts. And a cider. I recommend them to you. Both have proved nourishing.'

I slop several spoonfuls of the grey mush into the bowl and fill the cup, then I eat and drink. Father Melachlin, I decide, has, as always, been truthful. The porridge, although lumpy, nutty even, and quite tasteless, is warm and filling, and the cider is hot and biting.

Father Melachlin picks up a handful of pebbles and, one by one, in the gentlest of fashions, tosses them at the backs of my brethren. Each of them shifts and squirms in their slumber.

'It is better that they think they have awoken themselves,' says the Father. 'I would rather not make myself unpopular by acting like a cockerel ... And you, Brother Niall? Did you sleep?'

'Yes, I did, thank you, Father,' I reply. 'The women preparing the body were chanting. It did not take long for me to close my eyes.'

The Father laughs.

'And did you learn much?' he asks. 'About their rituals?'

'Nothing I would wish to remember,' I say.

I stutter for a moment.

'I was hoping,' I continue, 'that I might see something Christian or at least deeply spiritual about their practices. But instead it was as if they were preparing something for the spit.'

The good Father offers the barest of grimaces, which means ... something, I know not what ... and then,

29

studying the flames, he sinks into thought. There is something I must ask him, but I am unsure of which moment to choose.

'Dear Father,' I say eventually, and he looks up, catching my gaze fully and with compassion.

'What is it, my son?' he says.

'Father, I was wondering,' I say.

It is not often I question his thinking.

'I have been wondering,' I continue. 'I sense that you feel that this beast the Picts speak of does not actually exist. Am I right? If this is so, then surely it stands … Perhaps they may only be using the notion of the monster to hide something even more nefarious. Something of their own doing.'

Father Melachlin tosses another pebble towards Brother Aengus.

'Yes, I have had such thoughts myself,' he says. 'Whatever the Picts might tell us, it seems that the likelihood of some deadly creature inhabiting the loch is extremely small. It is far more likely that the poor man met his fate through other, more common, means. By the axe of one of his fellows, perhaps. But all that said, it is still probable that many of these people, most of them in fact, do believe in the beast. It will do our cause no harm, therefore, if we play along and continue to pretend that we, too, believe.'

'So when the time comes, Father?' I ask, 'how will we call upon the Lord? Will we pray? Or chant?'

'I,' says Father Melachlin. 'I have decided it is best that I alone should perform the rite. Therefore, if something should go wrong, this may in some small way protect the rest of you.'

'And what kind of rite will it be, Father?' I ask.

'An exorcism, I think,' says the Father with a laugh. 'I suppose you might call it an exorcism. Although I suspect it will be quite unlike any exorcism any of us might imagine.'

'Are you saying it will be feigned, Father?' I say. ' Just pretence?'

'Truly,' says Father Melachlin. 'It will be nothing more than a charade.'

'And have you considered, yet,' I ask, 'what form this exorcism will take?'

The Father laughs again.

'No, I have no idea, my son,' he says. 'What words will I speak about a monster from the deep? I have not given it much thought. Something about the perils of Jonah, perhaps. But it should not matter, Brother Niall. I will speak in Latin, a tongue far beyond any of these philistines. Just watch and learn. I will perform for them an exorcism the likes of which you have never seen. I will, by the grace of God, rid them of this non-existent beast forever. And then, if all goes to plan, we will be baptising in droves before the day is out.'

'But ... this fraudulence, Father?' I ask. 'Will not the good Lord disapprove of us practicing this deceit in his name?'

'I have faith the Lord will understand,' says the Father. 'This is one sure case in which the ends justify the means.'

THE PYRE

The fire is dying and the morning chill is at its worst. My brothers begin to rouse themselves and, rising, rub and scratch themselves. As one, they head for the line of trees that borders the village. But for Brother Eamon, I notice, who pours himself a cider.

'Did you sleep well, Brother?' I ask.

'Well enough,' he replies. 'Save for battling the elbows of my good Brother Aengus throughout the night.'

The cider is not to his taste. He discards what remains and, as the other brothers return, he, too, heads towards the trees for relief.

'Hurry yourselves, Brothers,' says Father Melachlin. 'The sun is close to rising and we have only moments before the funeral ceremony begins. Pagan as it might be, I think it is in our interest to attend. Eat and drink what you will and let us make our way.'

Each of my brothers enjoys a spoonful or two of porridge, but for Aengus, who enjoys several, and Father Melachlin leads us down to the shore of the loch. The Picts are beginning to gather and as the sky brightens, they begin to extinguish their torches.

Closer, we can see a structure of logs and branches. The corpse, now wrapped in what appears to be moistened linen, lies atop the logs.

We follow Father Melachlin's lead and, keeping our distance, gain a good vantage point some twenty yards from the pyre. The way the Picts are gathered, I can only assume that other than adding the flame, there will be no ritual or ceremony. They chatter amongst themselves and appear to offer the deceased no dignity or respect. Then, as the sun peeks out above the eastern hills, the woman, Domelch, steps forward and, taking the last torch from one of her tribesmen, holds it high in the air. For a moment, all is quiet. Then she shouts. Her tribesmen shout the same in reply.

'Caedmon is the word they speak,' says Brother Feargus. 'It must have been the warrior's name.'

The shouting continues, growing louder and louder, until, finally, the woman swings the torch and adds it to the pyre. In an instant, branches, logs, linen and body are in flames. Even from this distance, I feel the heat so intensely I must step back. I believe I can hear the basted skin of the body pop and crackle, like that of a roasted pig or goose. And I sense an odour in the air unlike any I have experienced before.

By now the mood has changed. The procession, the

behaviour of these Picts, has indeed become something much more base and carnal. In their excitement, perhaps affected by the odour, they appear to have entered a kind of delirium. Their shouting is now a chant and their motions have become dance-like. Together, they seem to have entered into some kind of trance. Soon they are shedding what few clothes they wear and are committing all manner of debauchery. It is enough to make all my brothers, myself included, grow concerned and look to Father Melachlin for advice. He alone amongst us seems undisturbed by the performance.

'Should we be watching this, Father?' I ask. 'I mean—'

He stops me with a firm hand on my shoulder.

'I understand what you are thinking my son,' he says. 'This ceremony, if we can call it that, is, even in the smallest sense, profane. You are afraid you may be drawn in. Especially by their nakedness. And by the lewd behaviour and indecent gyrations of their women.'

He knows me well. Better than I know myself. I am fearful my arousal is so strong it might show through the front of my habit.

'Do not despair,' Father Melachlin continues. 'If your faith is strong, as I know it is, you will overcome your desire to join them. You will see their actions as nothing more than sinful and barbaric.'

I accept what the good Father is saying. But even so, as I watch, I cannot help but take it to heart. These people, I feel, are truly living. They are accessing some

34

part of our Earthly experience that my brethren and I might only dream about.

The fire continues to burn and the revelling and chanting goes on. For over an hour, the Picts carouse and cavort, until, as the flames show the first sign of dying, they begin to quiesce. Their chanting becomes a murmur and, as if through exhaustion, many of them drop to their knees. And although many began their rite fully covered, most are now shamelessly naked. For many of my brethren, I believe it has been their first sight of a naked woman. For myself, I feel it is in my best interests to keep watching. It is important I take the most from the moment.

THE EXORCISM

Before long, there is nothing left to see. The pyre has burned away, leaving nothing more than a pile of smouldering ashes, and there is no sign of what was once the warrior, Caedmon. Even bones, I sense, would be hard to find, remaining only charred and fractured relics among the coals.

'So, Father?' I ask. 'Will you perform your exorcism now?'

'Shortly,' the Father replies. 'Even though mine will be but a performance, in God's name I believe it is better to let some time pass. No petition to our Lord, neither false nor sincere, should follow so close to this barbarity. We will let the fire die completely and allow the Picts a chance to return to their normal senses.'

'And have you considered any further, Father,' asks Brother Feargus, 'what form this exorcism will take?'

'No, I have still thought little about it,' says Father Melachlin. 'Save that my performance will be mostly invention. You must understand, my children, that it is not for the Lord I perform, but rather for these unsuspecting fools. My display is but a means to an end.'

It remains in my heart that the good Father may have crossed a line somewhere, that in seeking to deceive the Picts, he may, in some way, be corrupting the message of our Lord. But still, I say nothing. As the heathens split into smaller and smaller groups and Father Melachlin and the rest of my brethren wander back towards their fire, I join Brother Eamon. He alone amongst us has approached the pyre. He has his gaze fixed firmly on the ashes. He is concerned, I suspect, that this man, pagan though he may have been, now has no body to re-inhabit when our Lord returns.

'It all worries you, Brother?' I ask. 'I'm sure this cremation must have seemed an obscene act, an act of devilment, to someone so young. But rest easy. You are not alone, I can tell. Many of our brethren, too, have been deeply affected by the burning, by the profane nature of the rite.'

'Yes, I could not help but find it confronting, Brother Niall,' says Eamon.

But his tone surprises me a little. He seems remarkably calm and self-assured.

'But I do not believe for a moment we should judge these people,' he continues. 'Shun their barbarity, yes, but judge them, no. The act of burning the dead was one practised by our own folk in the times before Saint Patrick brought us the Word.'

I am forever surprised by the depth of knowledge in someone so young.

'Yes,' I say. 'I understand. But all the dancing ... The chanting ... The ... Surely you were unnerved by the whole performance.'

'Of course,' says Brother Eamon. 'But, again, it was much as I expected. What I truly fail to understand is why our Father Melachlin wishes to indulge these people such. I recognise that he wishes to baptise them into our faith, but I feel that no matter how much baptising is done, in their hearts, they will always remain barbarians.'

'Perhaps so,' I say. 'You may be right. But I believe it is not our task to question. It is our duty to follow. Come. It will not be long before the exorcism begins. Let us join the others.'

Our brethren are gathered around the fire in the centre of the village. Father Melachlin remains some distance apart. He is on his knees, eyes closed, muttering, fingering his rosary. We watch him and I think to myself. Even if the old man's actions hold no truth and are just a performance to prey on the gullibility of these heathens, they are impressive. And convincing. Many of the Picts have gathered around him and are watching him pray. I can tell by their faces they are befuddled, unsure what to make of him.

After a few moments, the crowd parts and the woman, Domelch, approaches. She, too, watches the Father. I expect her to interrupt his thoughts, but she does not. She holds her tongue until he opens his eyes and lifts his head.

'Are you ready now, priest?' Feargus translates. 'It is time to do as you promised. To rid us of the monster. Or shall we feed it one or two of your followers instead?'

'There is no need for that,' says the Father. 'I will do as I promised. But remember. As I have said, I expect something in return. If I do indeed rid the loch of its monster, I expect that your people, yourself included, will accept the power of our Lord and choose to follow his teachings.'

Feargus listens to the woman and then speaks again.

'She claims she is not one for making bargains,' he says. 'But she has decided that if you are at all success-ful, if we do not see the monster's return within, say, the next seven days, then, yes, she will accept that our Lord must indeed be powerful.'

Feargus takes a deep breath before continuing.

'But be warned,' he says. 'She says if you should fail, if the beast returns within these seven days ... then she will conclude that you have wasted her time. And the deception you have provided her people will not go unpunished. Some of us may end up continuing on our way, but she cannot guarantee that any of us will remain complete in body or in spirit.'

Feargus stops again and wipes his clammy hands upon his habit.

'Now, come, she says,' he continues. 'Perform your ceremony, before her patience thins even more and she does the monster's work herself. She says your head would not be out of place hanging in her hut or from her belt.'

Father Melachlin lifts his staff and uses it to get to his feet and begins his walk towards the loch. The Picts clear a pathway and, although unprompted, we dozen follow the Father closely towards the water. Never having witnessed such an event, an exorcism, pretend or otherwise, my brothers and I have no idea what to expect. Like the Picts, then, we are astonished when Father Melachlin stretches his arms and, at the top of his voice, begins to bellow.

'*Monstrum!*' he cries, and I feel my body quiver. '*Monstrum! Diabolical abyssi! Invoco te in nomine domini nostri Jesu Christi ut exeas de lacu isto ut exeas in pace istos homines et nunquam revertar!*'

Then, to the surprise of us all, Picts and novices included, he takes a bold step into the icy water. In he wades, until he stands waist-deep in the murky drink. I wonder to myself. Where does he get the strength, the will, to endure such cold? And, to be honest, the thought does cross my mind. As the good Father moves into the loch, I half-expect the monster, fictional as it is, to rise from it and, most likely, take more than his head. But the surface of the water remains still, until Father Melachlin begins thrashing his staff against it.

'*Abi bestia!*' he continues. '*Abi bestia! Abscede! Praecipio tibi in nomine Domini Dei nostri, ut revertaris ad inferos, unde venisti!*'

Some of the Picts are laughing, amused as they are at what must seem an absurd performance. Some of my brethren, too, are lost, clearly confused by an act unlike anything they have seen before. But the woman, Domelch, and those close to her, watch with interest. There is something about the Father's ritual, something in his words and actions, perhaps even in his message, that penetrates their minds, that I believe they are considering useful. But I do not believe for a moment they are taken in, that they are, for any small moment, prepared to follow in our Lord's path. I think it much more likely that they see an opportunity to extend their power over their people.

With a flourish, Father Melachlin swings his staff one last time, then he turns and slides from the black depth. And, although he must be freezing, he does not show it. At a gentle pace, he pushes his way through the crowd of Picts and approaches the central fire. My brethren and I follow him and huddle around.

'Are they watching me?' he asks. He lifts the front of his habit for a moment and sighs. 'Are their eyes upon me?'

'Yes, Father,' I say. 'You have certainly caught their interest. But … I can see your need to warm yourself, but … Are you not absolutely frigid? I have drunk from the loch. I have felt its icy surface. I know how cold it is.'

'As you might tell,' the Father says, 'I am indeed cold. I am so cold my balls are blue and have shrivelled up back inside me. I am lucky I have no use for them. But I feel it might harm us if I show weakness. Tell me. The woman. Where is she? Does she watch us?'

'Yes,' I say. 'In fact, she is approaching.'

The good Father drops his habit and rubs his hands.

'It is time, then,' he says, 'to see if my stratagem has worked. Tell me, Brother Niall. Was my performance convincing?'

'I believe it was, Father,' I say. 'I could read the faces of the Picts as they watched.'

'Perhaps you could,' says Father Melachlin. 'But I sense that it is her opinion that matters. We will have our answer momentarily.'

Truly, in that moment, the woman is beside us. She slaps the Father's shoulder and with her mighty hand takes a firm grasp of his buttock.

'Tell him,' she says to Brother Feargus. 'It was a fine performance, priest. If nothing else, I'm sure it will scare away the fishes.'

Feargus does as commanded.

'My part of the agreement is now complete,' Father Melachlin replies. 'I have banished the beast. All that remains is for you and your people to accept our Lord.'

'All in good time,' says Domelch. 'As I have said, we need time to see if your words have indeed succeeded. If, perhaps in six or seven days, the monster has not returned, then we might indeed accept that your God is a powerful one. If not, you will make the monster a fine meal.'

'It is as we agreed,' says the Father. 'But in the meantime? You expect us to—'

'Make your camp with us?' says the woman. 'Yes. I expect as much. But do not despair. We will keep you and your followers warm and well fed. And we will happily allow you to preach your faith. If in your waiting time you manage to convert some of my tribesmen, so much the better for you.'

'Are you certain, Father?' I hear Eamon whisper. 'Are you absolutely certain this monster does not exist? If we learn that there is indeed some kind of creature in the loch and your exorcism has not worked, it may be the end of us all.'

'Your lack of faith surprises me, Brother Eamon,' says Father Melachlin. 'The Lord will keep us safe. But if you are concerned for your safety, I shall ask. If some of us agree to stay here in this village, then perhaps the woman might allow the rest of you to leave. To preach to any people who may live further up the loch. Brother Feargus, pray, ask her. Ask her, say, if you and I remain here, will she allow some of the others to journey further up the loch to continue our mission?'

Feargus translates and we await the woman's answer.

'Two,' Feargus says. 'She says but two of us may leave. Some of her people are about to depart on a trading trip and she will allow two of us to accompany them. But she warns. We will find the trading trip ten times more dangerous than a quiet week here in their camp.'

'I leave it up to you, then, Brother Eamon,' says the Father. 'Since you were the first to broach the subject, I will leave it to you to decide. Will you stay or will you step out there into the unknown? But I caution you. I feel you are about to choose the worst of options.'

'It may be hazardous, Father,' says Eamon. 'But despite the danger, I feel an adventure will be easier than sitting around waiting for an axe to fall.'

'That is fair comment, Brother,' says Father Melachlin. 'I will do nothing to dissuade you. But tell me. If you were to choose a companion, who would it be? Brother Aengus? He could do with the exercise.'

'No, Father,' says Eamon. 'I would take Brother Niall. He is fit and brave and I believe he will offer good conversation along the way.'

I am thankful somehow for the choice made by my young brother.

'Make it so, then,' says the Father. 'Make yourselves ready. Come to me later and I will clarify your mission.'

WE DEPART ON OUR MISSION

There will be eight of us travelling – six Picts, all men, Brother Eamon and myself. We will travel along the loch's edge for a day or two. The Picts will carry pelts and all manner of dried and salted foods, to trade, we are told, for the metal tools – mostly blades and axes – and fine jewellery crafted in the next village.

The settlement we are presently in is too small for any major production, but we need only glance at the delicately carved and bejewelled broaches on the tunics and at the shining chains hanging around the necks of the people here to appreciate the level of craftsmanship of which some of their kind are capable. I find myself continually surprised. Especially as the Picts seem so otherwise ignorant. They have no books nor scrolls, in fact no written communication to speak of, and appear to be limited just to the crude carvings on the stones surrounding their village.

Father Melachlin has instructed us to remain close to our team of Picts, to maintain a constant level of prayer and, where possible, to try to gain their interest. This will not be easy. As Brother Feargus will remain in the camp with the others, we will have no way of communicating our intentions. We will be like ducks conversing with goats. Also, when we reach the next village, the good Father expects us to continue our proselytising there. If unsuccessful, he desires us to at least prepare the way for the others. Once again, I will be happy enough to escape with my head still attached and my gizzards still with me.

Even with their heavy packs upon their shoulders, the Picts make a good and steady pace. They chant or sing something in their vulgar tongue, something neither Eamon nor I can understand.

'Do you know much Latin?' says Eamon. 'Perhaps we can sing and outdo them.'

'Hardly,' I say. 'There are six of them and they are loud.'

'Perhaps so,' says Eamon. 'But we will have the strength of the Lord in our voices. Shall we sing an *Our Father*?'

'Very well,' I say, and we begin, warbling at first, but growing more and more confident as the words emerge.

'*Pater Noster,*
qui es in caelis,
sanctificetur nomen tuum.
Adveniat regnum tuum.
Fiat voluntas tua,

sicut in caelo et in terra.'

Brother Eamon looks at me, grinning, but, in a instant, the delight on both our faces disappears. The trailing Pict turns and, drawing his sword, holds it tight against poor Eamon's neck. He mutters something, clearly a command to desist, which we quickly do. We understand none of his words, save for, I think, 'samhchair'. In our language, this word meant silence. I believe in theirs it means no different.

Eamon and I close our mouths. In truth, I think, it is just as if we were travelling with Father Melachlin, although the good Father did not threaten to slit our throats every time we spoke.

We continue on, doing all we can to keep up with the Picts. But even fully laden, they can easily outpace us. Each step increases the distance between us. Then, finally, as the sun begins to sink, we see them veer away from the loch. Clearly, they plan no chance evening encounters with the monster. We follow them, until they find a clearing at the edge of some woods, about five hundred yards from the loch. Here they make their camp. They unload their packs and while some remove foodstuffs from their store, others gather wood for a fire.

THE CAMP

One of the Picts reveals what seems to be a cut of beef, or perhaps venison, and, placing it on a nearby stone, he hacks it into meal-sized pieces. Each of them, in turn, takes a slice and, impaling it on a stick, holds it over the fire. Brother Eamon and I can do nothing but watch. The crackling of the fat reaches our ears and its smell accosts our noses. Then, to our surprise, the Pict flings two of the remaining scraps of meat in our direction. I catch mine, a small, gristly offering, but Eamon's hands are like fists and his lands in the dirt.

'I will come with you, if you wish,' I say. 'We can travel down to the loch and wash it.'

'No,' says Eamon. 'It is of no matter. I will dust it off.'

He brushes the dirt away as best he can, then we gather two long green branches from a nearby tree. Soon, our steaks are burning alongside those the Picts. Sitting so closely, it is no longer the steaks we can smell, but the Picts themselves. Clearly, bathing is something rarely practised among their kind.

Our steaks cooked, I follow Brother Eamon and take a position some distance away, out of range of the odour, but close enough that we might still benefit from the light and warmth of the fire. The sun has now set and the chill of the night is truly with us.

'We are lucky,' I say, 'that we still have all our own teeth. I have noticed. Many of these barbarians have empty mouths. Whether through fighting or bad hygiene, I cannot tell.'

'I had noticed,' says Brother Eamon. 'Many of them merely suck on their meat before throwing what remains on the fire. Others gnash on it like a cow on its cud.'

We laugh, and bite. Our meat is tough, and over-cooked, but we have not eaten since our morning porridge. I am not sure Eamon ate even then, so we continue until all but the gristle is in our bellies. Then we sit and watch and wait for the Picts to settle into their night's rest. They will, I hope, leave a space for us close to the fire.

They don't. They chatter and laugh amongst themselves, then, in an hour or so, the six of them spread out, their arses inward, circling the fire in the neatest of rings. Each holds his sword or his axe to his chest, no doubt as a first defence against any attack. I consider joining them, but one look to Brother Eamon confirms my thoughts. These Picts would show no patience. Were

Eamon or I to approach, just the slightest snap of a twig might see the end of us.

'Should we risk another fire?' says Eamon.

'If only we knew how to light one,' I say. 'No, I think we are in for a cold night. All we can do is approach as close as we dare and ask the Lord for his warmth.'

So we do. Making our movements as obvious as we can, we go about gathering handfuls of loose heather, then, approaching to within a dozen or so feet from the Picts, we make our beds. Our heads lie close and I cannot help but wonder. Is this honeysuckle that I smell or just the scent of the heather? Or can it be that Brother Eamon has washed his hair?

I struggle to gain any sleep. Not only disturbed by the cold and by Eamon's gentle breaths, I lie in fear of an attack by some unknown assailant or of being torn apart by a wandering beast. When the moon is still high, I decide to rise. I leave Brother Eamon to his slumber and risk an approach to the Picts and the now smouldering fire. Close, I catch the eye of two of the Picts. Clearly, they too have been sleeping lightly. I receive a pair of cold, almost murderous glares, but they make no move towards me. If anything, they shift away, offering me a clear path between them. I squeeze between their bodies and approach the fire. I get to my knees, feeling the glow on my face and hands. After a moment, I stand and, turning my arse to the embers, I lift my habit.

The Picts have not moved. They are not, it seems, as hazardous to my health as I had imagined. Part of me, in truth, feels more secure inside their ring of iron. But, despite the comfort I feel, I worry about Eamon, still sleeping alone some distance away. From where I stand, I can see his outline against the bushes beyond. As far as I can tell, he has not moved since our heads hit the heather. I believe he must have been asleep before I had counted even a dozen or so sheep. I envy the simplicity and naivety of his youth. But with his soft locks, bright blue eyes and slim form, I believe he is too pretty for a boy. Far too much so, I have decided. I believe he is yet to put a razor to his face.

My arse now warm, scalded even, I head back towards him, my only concern that I accidentally kick one of the Picts as I pass. An event such as that, I decide, will surely test their good nature. But I manage to pass without incident and, within moments, I have rejoined Brother Eamon. I sit myself in the heather alongside him and watch him sleep.

'You are restless, Brother?' I hear.

His voice surprises me. I had imagined him deep in slumber.

'A little,' I say. 'But I was cold, also. I thought I might risk the wrath of those heathens to warm myself. But you? I had imagined you were sleeping soundly.'

'Not quite,' says Eamon. 'I, too, have been restless.'

He sits up and crosses his legs, his knees almost touching mine.

'I have been wondering,' he continues, 'what awaits us tomorrow. If and when we reach this new village. I cannot help but wonder how we are to fulfil the task

Father Melachlin has given us. Surely we will need a miracle in order to minister to them.'

'Especially,' I say, 'since we have no shared language. We will be as well speaking in tongues.'

'But perhaps,' says Brother Eamon. 'Perhaps we should not give it thought. As the good Father often says, the Lord may show us the way.'

'Truly,' I say. 'But it seems to me. Perhaps we rely on the Lord just a little too often.'

'This monster,' says Eamon. 'This monster they are all in fear of. Do you believe it actually exists?'

'I have my doubts,' I say. 'Grave doubts. As does Father Melachlin. But I also think it serves us no purpose to make the Picts aware of this. It is far better, until we are free of this tribe, to maintain the image that we are in as mortal fear as they are.'

Even in the darkness, I can see that Eamon is cold. He rubs his arms and legs persistently and slaps his arms across his chest. Poor boy, I think to myself. I am certain he lacks the courage to cross the line of barbarians and approach the fire. That said, I can feel the fire's effect on my own body beginning to wane. My bones themselves are beginning to chill. Were it not unseemly, I would suggest to Brother Eamon that we might embrace each other. By holding each other close, we might draw on the heat that remains in each other's bodies. But I accept that such behaviour, even the suggestion of it, is inappropriate and undignified. So each of us, in turn, huddles into our pile of heather again and closes our eyes.

THE SECOND DAY

No sooner do we settle back down than the pagans begin to stir. First one then another rises until all six, having performed their ablutions, begin to gather their packs. The smallest, but also the loudest of the six, approaches me and, without warning, delivers a solid kick to my belly. He shouts something unintelligible, yet something I can easily interpret. I shake Brother Eamon and the two of us rise.

It is clear this time there will be no breakfast. Even since my nighttime visit, the fire has died down to nothing. If we desire anything to fill our bellies, I can tell we will be picking berries and chewing grass seeds along the way. But we have no time to consider our options. As the sun begins to rise over the soft hills in the east, the Picts are already beginning their path towards it. They follow the narrowest of tracks that leads both towards the rising sun and back to the loch.

It is not long before we reach the loch and begin to

traverse our familiar path alongside its bank. As usual, the Picts show no willingness to wait for us and for most of the morning, my brother and I must work beyond our usual pace in order to keep up. By noon, when the sun is at its zenith and the Picts finally show signs of stopping for a break, Eamon and I are close to exhaustion. While the Picts drink heartily from the loch, my brother and I collapse in the shade of the nearest tree.

Brother Eamon is breathing heavily; his face is flushed and sweat drips down his cheeks and neck. Even with a little rest, I doubt he can go much further. I can only hope our trek will soon be over.

To my own surprise, I find myself wiping the sweat from his brow and offering him some comfort by fanning him with a bunch of leaves. Even so, he looks ready to faint.

'Hold still,' I say. 'I will borrow a cup or a bowl from the Picts and get you some water.'

I rise and head towards the loch and the Picts, but pressing my point is no easy task. The Picts, it seems, have no cups, in fact no receptacles of any kind. I must resort, using the most basic of sign language, to borrowing one of their helmets. A good rinse, I decide, and it will hold enough to sate the thirst of my poor brother. I first lay on the bank and drink my fill, before carrying the full helmet to Eamon. He drinks without stopping, draining the vessel in one attempt, and I can see he could easily do so again. I return to the loch and refill the helmet. That, sadly, is all I manage. The helmet is pulled rudely from my grip and the contents arc splashed in my face. The helmet's owner stands over me with a hurtful grin. He growls something at me, which of course I do not understand, then turns away to join his friends. It is clear that they have no desire to wait for us. I must rush to help Eamon to his feet, before offering him all the encouragement I can to follow the Picts. But I admit. The boy's resilience, the courage and determination he applies to his recovery, surprises me.

Yet, even with all of Brother Eamon's inner strength, it is not long before a sizeable distance has opened up between us and the Picts. So much so that as they pass around one corner then another, we find them disappearing completely from view. And as they tread so lightly, there is no sign of their footsteps in the turf close to the loch. I can only hope that by sticking by the water's edge, we will remain in their path.

'Do you need to stop, Brother?' I ask Eamon. I can feel his weight on my shoulder.

'No, let us press on,' he says. 'I will rest when the time is right.'

So we continue, with no company and no way of knowing which, if any way, is correct, until the afternoon is close to ending. The Picts, I am sure, are long gone, probably miles ahead, thankful they have left us troublesome priests behind.

Then, when there seems nothing much else to do but give up for the day, perhaps try our luck at catching a fish or two for nourishment, we hear them. Over the rise before us comes the unmistakable sound of human voices. They are in the Pictish tongue, but in our present state, they come like the honeyed songs of angels.

'Can you manage, brother?' I ask, but Eamon has already pulled free of my grip and is pressing his way up the rise. I follow quickly in his path.

WE REACH THE SECOND VILLAGE

F rom the top of the rise we can see a settlement, larger than the first, with perhaps fifty or so dwellings and at least two or three hundred inhabitants. The place is alive with activity, with a number of market stalls and what seems to be an iron smelter at work. Our own Picts, if we can call them that, stand in the central clearing. They are engaging with several of the locals, laughing and drinking what I can only assume is something alcoholic and heady. They seem relaxed and trusting of their hosts.

'Do we risk approaching?' says Eamon.

'I feel we have little choice,' I say. 'We will not last long out here by ourselves. And besides, we must not forget the task Father Melachlin has imposed on us. Come, we shall go together.'

With slow but steady steps, we sink down the hill's decline and head towards the settlement. First one, then another of the town's inhabitants stops and stares at us.

They stare at us as oddities, as curiosities they might not have seen before. Then our own band of Picts catch sight of us. Their response towards our obvious exhaustion, our tired and weary appearance, is laughter. I can feel my cheeks burn. Soon all of those who can see us are also laughing. I feel Brother Eamon's hand grasp for mine. This has become a common event in times such as this.

I offer what unspoken comfort I can and pull him towards the Picts.

'Come, Eamon,' I say. 'There is nothing we can do but face them.'

It is as if, from the moment we landed in this infernal country, our lives have been in danger. From the elements, from the terrain, from these unforgiving inhabitants, I have felt threats at every turn. Even now, as we inch forward, all I see are glares and snarls and hands fingering blades.

We have taken but a few steps into the village before I hear even more laughter. But this time, I cannot be mistaken, it is accompanied by the sound of words in our own language. I look around and see, appearing from within the crowd, an old man. He reminds me, at first glance, of Father Melachlin, although his hair and beard are longer and even more bedraggled. And rather than a habit, he wears the conventional attire of the Picts, barely a loincloth under his fat, rolling belly. But I notice a wooden crucifix hanging from his neck.

It seems logical that we approach him.

'My name is Brother Niall,' I say. 'I am one of a brotherhood of monks from Killeaney in Hibernia. This is Brother Eamon. We are here to deliver the Word of the Lord to these people.'

'Yes, so I have gathered,' says the man. 'Well, good luck to you. I've been doing just that for the past fifteen years and you can see where it has gotten me. Now I am more like them than anything. I was once Father Cillian. I was a Hibernian monk like you. But you may call me Cruinn. It is their name for me now. It has something to do with this.'

He slaps his belly.

'When in Rome, we do as the Romans, eh?' he says.

He pulls a young woman out from the crowd.

'And this is Eithni, my wife,' he says.

They kiss, lasciviously, and Eamon and I look uneasily at each other.

'You are both as well coming to terms and finding a woman for yourselves,' the man says. 'You will find that there is no going back, either to Hibernia or to the celibate life. Or do you boys have a hankering for each other? I sense some chemistry between you.'

I quickly decide that Eamon is now strong enough to support himself and I let him go. He wobbles momentarily before leaning against the nearest hut and removing a sandal. A pulse of blood flows from the sizeable blisters that cover the sole of his left foot.

'My, Eamon,' I scold. 'You should have said something. We could have stopped. We might have found a way of tending these wounds.'

'Only for us to lose the Picts entirely?' says Eamon.

'No, that would have solved nothing. And besides, I have suffered from these swellings for several days now, since long before we arrived at that last village. They are something I have gotten used to.'

'I must wonder, then,' I say, 'why you were so quick to volunteer for this mission. You could at this very moment be back resting with Father Melachlin and the others.'

'I would have found that rest tiresome enough,' says Eamon. 'No. So long as my teeth have remained clenched and my eyes have been focused on the horizon, I have found the blisters bearable enough.'

'Even so,' I say. 'Stop touching them. You will only make them worse. Hold still ... Cruinn, am I wrong? I am sure these heathen will have something, some balm, some lotion or potion, that will ease the pain and help the healing.'

'Do you think that because they are not Christian, they are ignorant?' says Cruinn. 'That they have no knowledge of medicine or healing? The truth is quite the opposite. They have come to learn much from Mother Nature and have much, in turn, to teach. They are not so quick to dismiss her teachings as you might be. Here, this is our hut. Come inside. We can treat him better there.'

I offer Eamon my shoulder and assist him, shuffling, into the gloom of Cruinn's hut. The old man follows with a torch.

CRUINN'S HUT

While the torch offers us little illumination, I find my eyes adapting quickly to the lack of light. Cruinn gets to his knees, slowly, and examines Eamon's foot.

'Your feet are small,' he says. 'Even for a boy of your age. They are poorly made for long treks such as you have undertaken.'

I interrupt him.

'So, Cruinn?' I ask. 'Are you, truly, a man of God?'

'I am ... or at least I was,' says Cruinn. He says something to his wife in the pagan tongue and she departs.

'I came from Croher a long, long time since,' he continues. 'With my brethren on what I assume is the same task as yours. But we found it a pointless exercise. As I am sure you will. Now, my followers are all dead and I have become as heathen as any of this rabble.'

'But our Father Melachlin,' I say. 'Further down the

loch. He has been successful. At least in part. He has been preaching the Lord's Word and is, at this very moment, baptising a village full of these natives.'

Cruinn looks at me with a grin.

'That seems unlikely,' he says. 'And how did he manage it? With sorcery?'

Perhaps, I think to myself, but I answer with a straight face.

'He has performed an exorcism,' I say. 'And rid the village of a great beast that has been raiding and killing its warriors.'

Cruinn grins again, this time wider.

'Ah, the monster,' he says. 'Yes, I'm very familiar with its deeds. But if it were only so easy. The people here have looked to me to perform such hocus pocus to rid them of it. And it may seem to work for a time. But your Father Melachlin will soon find out. This monster will return and the heathens will quickly return to their old ways. It seems, in the end, that they would rather have their warriors go off to engage the beast in mortal combat. But, so far, only corpses have returned, drifting down the loch like rafts upon the River Styx. Headless, limbless, in all fashion of mutilation. You need only look out there to see the monster's latest work. Three more of this village's finest warriors have gone to battle the beast, only to return battered and broken.'

Truly, as I peer outside the hut, I see, in the middle of the village, the bodies of three Pictish men in all manner of disfigurement.

'But this monster?' I ask. 'Is it actually real? Our Father Melachlin had no doubt. He seemed to believe it was but a figment, a product of heathen superstition.'

'Oh, have no doubt,' says Cruinn. 'It is real. As real as any beast you might find in the field or fish you might find in the sea.'

Eithni returns with a basket. Even in the darkness, I can see it is filled with leaves. I can sense their sweet apple-like aroma. Also in the basket are some strips of linen and what appears to be a mortar containing a paste-like substance. Eithni places the basket beside Cruinn and, after brushing the dirt from Eamon's foot, the old man proceeds to apply some of the ointment.

'What is that?' I ask.

'Nothing magical, if that is your worry,' says Cruinn. 'Mostly a mix of honey and lemon. It will serve to ward off infection. And the leaves, if you are curious, are mostly chamomile. They will both ease the pain and hasten the healing of the wounds. Even by morning, your young friend here should feel an improvement.'

We watch as he presses the leaves to Eamon's foot and then tightly wraps the linen. He squeezes the foot back into its sandal, then, wiping his sticky hands on Eamon's habit, he stands.

'Tell me, Cruinn,' I say. 'The dead warriors ... I can see activity there. Will there be another funeral tomorrow?'

'Not tomorrow, but tonight,' says Cruinn. 'They have decided not to wait. It will begin as soon as the sun sets.'

'And will there be intoxication?' I ask. 'And fornication? We saw such a rite at the previous village. I know I am only still a novice, but I have never in my time seen a display of such barbarism.'

'Truly?' says Cruinn. 'And at this other village? Did any of the women approach you? To try to have their way with you?'

'My Lord,' I say. 'Thankfully, no.'

'I am surprised,' says Cruinn. 'With all the strange substances they consume, they often cannot resist their desires. Men and women both. They will mate with anything, even puny morsels like you. You were lucky you came in a pack. They no doubt considered themselves outnumbered. Here, the two of you will be easy pickings. The moon will have barely risen before each of you will have been ridden by half a dozen of those women. And by some of the men, as well, if I'm not mistaken.'

I look to Eamon. His face is pale and I can see his hands trembling as much as mine.

'But our vows,' I say. 'What can we do?'

'I can see only two ways,' says Cruinn. 'Either you forget all about your vows and join in. You never know. You may even enjoy yourselves. Or, if that is not to your taste, I suggest you put some distance between yourselves and the village before nightfall. You still have some time before the sun sets. Just remember, though, that in their heightened state, these heathen will search high and low for release.'

'How far need we travel, Cruinn?' I ask.

'Not to the ends of the Earth, if that is your fear,' says Cruinn. 'I think but a mile or so should see you safe enough.'

I look to Eamon again, and to his bandaged foot.

'Do you think you can walk that far?' I ask. 'If not, I will arm myself with a weapon of some sort. I will readily defend us.'

'No, that is not necessary, Brother,' says Eamon. 'I am sure I can walk, albeit slowly. But collect what you would use as a weapon and I will use it as a staff ... And Father Cillian, if you will? Can you assist us in gaining some food before we leave? We have eaten little since yesterday and I can feel the Devil's claws at my belly.'

'I am sure we can find you something,' says Cruinn. 'Some soup or a bone to chew on. Unlike most of these heathens, I see you still have your own teeth. Just wait. I will see what we can do.'

Once again, he says something to his wife and, once again, like an obedient servant, she scurries off.

'So where ...?' says Eamon. 'Where can we go? Is there somewhere safe nearby? Somewhere that might offer us some shelter from the elements?'

The old man thinks hard for a moment before replying.

'Yes, there is a place,' he says. 'If you continue along the edge of the loch for a mile or so, you will come upon a set of caves. The largest of these will protect you, not only from the night air and the hands and desires of these pagan maidens, but from the searching eyes of the monster of the loch.'

Eamon is listening closely.

'Will you be able to walk that far?' I ask.

'For certain,' he says. 'Do not worry. If the ground is flat and without stones, I am sure I will manage.'

'Good,' says the old man. He laughs, from somewhere deep and carnal. 'I would happily show you the place myself, but I am not so old as to eliminate myself from tonight's cavorting. I shall be participating along with the rest of the village. But look. Here is Eithni with your meal. Enjoy it as if it is your last.'

The woman hands each of us a bowl. This time, there is little meat, but the broth is hot and tasty. We drink it quickly. It takes us only moments to empty our bowls. We return them to Eithni and, with a little difficulty, I help Eamon to his feet.

'Are you sure you would not prefer,' I ask, 'to hide in the underbrush a little less distant from the village? If we hide ourselves well, we might easily go undetected.'

'No, I would rather not,' says Eamon. 'I do not wish to take the chance. I would much rather put some real distance between us and this evil. And these caves Cruinn has mentioned sound like the perfect shelter. Come, give me your shoulder to lean on. We have at least an hour yet before nightfall. I am sure, if we make unhindered progress, we should reach the caves by then.'

I lean in and welcome Eamon's arm over my shoulders and, with his makeshift staff in his other hand, we shuffle out of the hut. I can feel every wince that Eamon makes as his left foot hits the ground.

'I trust you will survive the night,' says Cruinn with a laugh. 'And not become an evening snack for the beast of the loch. And do not despair. Providing no one else is taken in the night, it will be safe enough for you to return in the morning.'

WE LEAVE THE VILLAGE

S o we head off, through the centre of the village and under the critical gaze of its inhabitants, until we reach a long stretch of open grassland. The sun is still warm on our backs and as we move away from the chatter of the villagers, we return to a place of peace and tranquility. Eamon is very much favouring his wounded foot, so I do not force him. We sink into a gentle motion and I allow him, on occasion, to pause and recover his strength.

It is not long before we have left the village well behind us and the only music to our ears is the lapping of the waves on the shore of the loch. Nevertheless, I can still sense that Eamon finds the going hard. I decide to engage him in conversation, hoping that a few words might take his mind from his pain.

'I have realised,' I say. 'Although we have been close enough these past few weeks, we really know very little about each other. Is it true, Brother Eamon, that you are the son of royalty? What a luxurious upbringing you must have had. Much different from this.'

Eamon breaks into a laugh and it is a joy to see him smile.

'Not so luxurious,' he says. 'I am only the second son of a second son. By the time the wealth filtered down, there was not much left for such as I. But this was probably a blessing. It gave me the opportunity to study. Our village was not far from the monastery at Tara and the monks there welcomed the opportunity to teach me. They taught me not only the scriptures, but the wisdom of the ancients, too. The Greeks, such as Pythagoras, Plato and Aristotle, were a frequent part of my reading.'

I listen closely, but the truth is, these names mean little to me. They are as well being the names of sheep in the field.

'And you?' says Eamon. 'Have you read much?'

It pleases me that his gait has changed and he is willing to engage in conversation, but it embarrasses me that, in comparison, I am but an ignorant yokel.

'No, I'm afraid my education was somewhat poor,' I say. 'I was fourteen years of age before I had even seen a book or a scroll. But for the goodwill and wisdom of Father Melachlin, I would be as ignorant even now ... Perhaps ... Perhaps when this ordeal is over, you might offer me some tutoring.'

'Willingly,' says Eamon. 'You may be surprised, Niall, but I have found that reading beyond the Lord's Word does much to open the mind. It has made me realise. There is much to life beyond the scriptures. But I fear that, between the Picts and the monster, our chances of ever returning to Hibernia alive are small.'

He laughs again. I know it is the only fitting response to such doubts.

'I am not so pessimistic,' I say. 'I am sure the Lord will continue to protect us. As he continues to guide us on his path.'

'Of that I am not so sure,' says Eamon. 'Father Melachlin did, after all, send us on a task. But we have done nothing yet to proselytise in the village.'

'But I am confused,' I say. 'If you find reading beyond the scriptures so appealing, why is it you choose to remain in the order? Why do you not step into the world and explore what it has to offer?'

'For precisely that reason,' says Eamon. 'I have a love of scripture, holy or otherwise, and it is in the monasteries where the books and scrolls are to be found. For good or ill, the Church has chosen to protect the common people from such knowledge. It is only as a monk that I might have access.'

I feel the chill in the air well before the sun goes down. I feel, too, the goosebumps on my brother's forearm. It seems that neither of us is prepared for the cold of the night.

'We have erred, Eamon,' I say. 'We have neglected to bring a flint. Unless fortune blesses us, we will be without a fire this night.'

'I had considered as much,' says Eamon. 'I have been keeping my eyes to the ground. But as much as my feet welcome the soft surface, my sight is yet to include a suitable fire starter.'

THE CAVE

S o we walk on, until, thankfully, just as the sun reaches the horizon behind us, we come upon a rocky outcrop. It takes us only minutes more to discover the promised cave. Its opening is tall and wide and, in the darkness, we cannot see where its depths might end.

'Rest here, brother,' I say, helping Eamon down onto a large boulder. 'Although the depths of the cave may bring us safety, I am a little afraid of the unknown. Despite what dangers may come from outside, I think it is best that we sleep close to the mouth of the cave. While this little light persists, I shall gather some branches and do my best to hide us from any passers by.'

'I understand,' says Eamon. 'Whether by bats or by bears, I have no keen wish to be roused from my dreams.'

There are several fallen branches from the trees nearby and it does not take long for me to build some camouflage around our enclosure. But as I work, I cannot but notice. The stench my body emits is worse than that of the Picts. It seems days since I properly bathed.

'Eamon, the waters of the loch are cold,' I say. 'But not so cold that we cannot wash. What say you we immerse ourselves? We can get the dousing done quickly.'

'Perhaps tomorrow,' says Eamon. 'Not tonight. I am cold enough already.'

So I bathe alone. I strip off my habit and, ever aware that the current might reach for me and take me away, I step gingerly into the loch. But the water is freezing. Immediately, I have renewed respect for the hardiness of our dear Father Melachlin. And I understand, too, why bathing for the Picts is the rarest of activities. So I stand on the shore and, using a handful of wet heather as a kind of soap, I scrub myself thoroughly and vigorously, until the smell of sweat has gone.

'Are you sure?' I ask Eamon, offering him a fresh clump of heather. But the boy has averted his eyes. If I did not know better, I would say he is ashamed at the sight of my nakedness. So I slip on my habit again and rest on the boulder beside him. I notice immediately that, while I have bathed, he has been busy, too, creating a bed for us of heather and moss.

'I imagine you are tired,' I say, as we settle in. 'It has been a difficult few days.'

'No, not tired so much,' says Eamon. 'Sleep has not

been difficult. But I am bodily weary, yes. After all this walking is done, I fear I will need some time to recover.'

There is a part of me, a part unfamiliar, that is ready to offer to knead his tired muscles. But I must remind myself again that any such contact between brothers is not only frowned upon, it may even be considered sinful. So we sit in silence, in the darkness, waiting for the other to speak. We wait, also, for the unmistakable sounds of the village festivities. We are not so far away as to be out of hearing range of their chanting and music.

Sure enough, it is not long before we hear the beating of drums and the high-pitched wail of voices on edge. We sit there, still, as the pounding and chanting grows louder. Try as I might, I cannot escape from images of naked painted bodies, wild dancing and open fornication. I look into the darkness towards Eamon. I sense that he too is disturbed by the celebrations. I feel his hand close to mine and squeeze it.

'It bothers you?' I ask.

'Some,' he says, squeezing back. 'But I am sure I will survive it.'

'Don't worry,' I say. 'I have a feeling the old man was merely trying to frighten us. I am sure we are more than safe where we are. I consider it extremely unlikely any of the Picts will leave the village. It is even more unlikely they will wander this far up the loch, especially if they believe the monster is on the loose.'

I can tell that this does little to calm the boy.

'Please,' he says. 'Say no more. I was almost fine. I

had almost calmed myself until you mentioned the beast again.'

'I am sorry,' I say. 'I will speak no more of it. If it helps, I am sure we can do something else to calm our minds.'

'Like count sheep?' laughs Eamon. 'Or babble away in Latin until we feel nothing at all? No, I think we will need another way to drive these noises from our ears.'

'Perhaps, then, if we lie down and sleep,' I say. 'Although you say you are not tired, I am sure if you close your eyes, Morpheus will come quickly.'

'I thought you did not know the Greeks,' says Eamon.

'Not well,' I say. 'But I am not entirely ignorant.'

We shuffle about until each of us lies comfortably, me on my back and Eamon with his back to me. In what little light exists, before I close my eyes, I can see the outline of his narrow waist and rounded hips. I need all my will to force it from my thoughts that I find the boy attractive, in a way unbecoming to any man, let alone a monk. So I too turn away and, with Latin on my lips, I pray for sleep and then the dawn.

THE LONGEST NIGHT

I do not know for how long I sleep, but I awaken cold and shivering and, to my surprise, with Eamon pressed hard against my back. His arm hangs loose across my shoulder and his breath blows soft against my neck. I cannot tell if he has, in his sleep, merely sought me out for warmth or if he has made this move deliberately. In any case, I do not care. I am happy to lie here and enjoy both the familiarity and comfort he brings.

Then – it seems he does this without thought – his hand begins to move. It moves from my shoulder to my arm, then further, sliding slowly down the front of my habit until it reaches …

It is true. And I cannot help myself. Suddenly, I feel myself stiffen and willing to submit to whatever sin might befall me. Without thinking, I find myself rolling onto my back and surrendering to the boy's desires.

I feel Eamon's fingers inching lower. Then, as they

reach the hem of my habit and slide beneath, I feel the hairs on my legs begin to tingle. My manhood, hard and proud, feels fit to explode. I know for certain now that the boy is awake. And I wonder. I know that this was a common practice among the Greeks, but I am surprised that Eamon has taken them so much to heart.

I open my mouth to speak, but he hushes me. I can do naught then but shiver, as his fingers reach their goal and he begins to stroke me, up and down, slowly, with a touch both delicate and firm. His nails dig lightly into my sack before crawling their way up my swollen member. Then, his actions quicken, as if he has planned for me some majestic release. But no. Each time as I draw close, I feel him relax to let my passion subside. It is a gentle, endless torture.

Now, if I am not astonished enough, I feel him shift. He moves closer, and lower, and then slips his head beneath the cover of my habit. Once again, I can do nothing but tremble, as sweet young Eamon, this boy I have known for but days, takes me deep inside his mouth. I feel his tongue run softly along the length of my shaft and, despite all the respect I hold for him and all my desire to prolong the ecstasy, I feel myself giving in. I feel my life energy spurt deep into the poor boy's throat.

But Eamon does not seem to mind. In fact, he licks the head of my now flaccid manhood clean before rising and resting his head upon my chest.

I feel an emotion wash over me. It is an emotion quite unlike anything I am used to. It is guilt. Of course, as someone used to following the Word of the Lord, I have felt guilt before, but not like this. This is not the guilt of simple transgression, of having sinned. Far from it. It is more, as I brush the boy's soft locks away from his face, the guilt of having used Eamon, of having not resisted his advances enough and, thus, of having taken advantage of him. Without, it seems, letting him share in my bliss. I now have no words. My only option, unaccustomed as I am and, truthfully, apprehensive about the deed, is to reciprocate, to perform for him the delightful act he has just performed for me. I shift myself lower and, as he has done, reach towards his bare legs and the contents of his habit.

He catches me by surprise as he takes my arm in a firm grip, pushing it away rather than drawing it closer.

'No,' he says. 'I would rather you did not.'

'But why?' I whisper. The only things listening are the tiny creatures in the cave. 'We have already broken so many of God's laws. It is only fair I give you even half the pleasure you have given me.'

'I thank you,' says Eamon. 'But I am content. Perhaps if I roll over, you might hold me. In that way we might find both comfort and warmth.'

I do as he asks and nestle closely into the grooves of his back. Once again, I can smell the scent in his hair. I find myself running my hand along his flank and, to my shame, I find myself aroused again. I can feel the stiffness of my manhood pressing hard between his buttocks.

'I am sorry,' I say. 'It is beyond my control.'

'I do not mind,' says Eamon. 'It assures me that you find me attractive. In fact ...'

With this, and without shifting his position, he reaches behind and pulls up my habit. He takes me in hand and begins to offer some long, slow, gentle strokes.

'Does this please you?' he asks.

'Very much,' I say.

'Good,' says Eamon. 'Then let us be quiet and embrace what remains of the night.'

I do as he commands and it is with Eamon bringing me to heaven once again that I finally feel sleep creep upon me. For the remains of the night, we are caught in a tight and warm embrace.

THE MIST ARRIVES

As comforting as the night is, when the dawn comes, I find myself cold again and alone. Eamon, it seems, has awakened early and abandoned me.

I stand and, brushing the heather and moss from my habit, push my way past the branches that still block the entrance to the cave. Outside, I find a thick mist has dropped over the loch and I can barely see the twenty feet from the cave to the shore.

'Eamon?' I call, more in hope than expectation. I cannot see him anywhere.

'I am here,' I hear his voice. As the breeze parts the mist momentarily, I see his outline. He is standing by the edge of the loch. I kneel and, in the briefest of motions, splash my face with the icy water.

'Come,' says Eamon. 'During my own bathing, I have managed to gather a breakfast of sorts.'

I stand and he passes me a handful of snails.

'They are quite tough,' he says, 'but nourishing enough. And as we have no way of catching fish or game, I suspect they will have to do.'

'You will not hear me complaining,' I say. I smash the first snail against a nearby rock and chew on its meat.

'It is still very cold,' I say, not sure what kind of conversation I might offer.

'It is the mist,' says Eamon. 'The dampness. I have only been out here a short while and between my bathing and the mist, my habit is soaked through.'

'Perhaps we should return to the cave, then,' I say. 'Staying here, the Devil might bring you down with any kind of ailment.'

'Perhaps he might,' says Eamon. 'But I feel I need the fresh air. At least for a short while. As secure as it was, I found the cave quite stuffy. The air, after a while, seemed stale.'

From what I can see, he is gazing out over the loch. As I chew on my snails, I watch him, lost for words and, in my own heart, lost for a definitive path back to the Lord. All is quiet. There is no sound from the village. All the sport and cavorting must be over and the villagers must be resting their aching heads. The only sound we can hear is the lap, lap, lapping of the tiny waves against the shore.

'Did you hear that?' whispers Eamon.

'Did I hear what?' I ask.

He presses his finger to his lips and grasps my arm tightly.

'Listen,' he says, and we move slowly back towards the mouth of the cave.

We listen and, presently, the sound becomes more and more audible. It is quite unlike any sound I have heard before. It is much like the lapping of the waves, but louder and more regular, as if something large is forcing its way through the water.

'Can you see anything, Brother?' I ask.

'Not really,' says Eamon.

But then, in an instant, our curiosities are answered. The mist is still thick, but just for a moment it lifts, to reveal ...

'Do my eyes deceive me, Brother?' I ask fearfully.

'No, Brother. They do not,' says Eamon.

It is our proof. There, creeping through the mist in the centre of the loch, is the beast itself. We can only see its head and neck, but it must protrude at least fifteen or twenty feet from the surface of the water. And even from this distance and through the mist, we can see the menace in its dragon-like form.

Then, as quickly as it has appeared, the creature disappears into the mist again. It is heading, I cannot help but consider, in the direction of the village and our friends, the Picts.

'Should we hurry?' Eamon asks. 'There may be a way we can reach the village first and warn them.'

'I think not,' I say. 'I think it sensible that we wait until the mist has lifted. I fear we may lose our way after only fifty yards or more. And I suspect that your foot, even if it has healed somewhat, will still hinder our progress. We may need to re-dress it before we leave.'

'Perhaps you are correct,' says Eamon.

His gaze is held by what has become again a blanket of white.

'But standing here does us no good,' I say. 'Come. Let us return to the shelter of the cave.'

I offer him my hand and lead him inside.

WE RETURN TO THE CAVE

The light here in the mouth of the cave is better now and we can see each other's faces. But as we sit on our pile of heather and moss, I can see the degree of saturation in Eamon's habit. His bathing as well as the mist have truly soaked him through and, try as he might to hide it, I can see him shivering. I am less than honest if I say my motives are purely honourable.

'I suggest you free yourself of the garment,' I say. 'It is doing you more harm than good. I think you should strip and hang your habit over those branches to dry.'

'I would rather not,' says Eamon. 'Even after our deeds last night, I do not wish for you to see me naked.'

'I will see you naked soon enough if you die,' I say. I stand and offer him my hand.

'Come. Disrobe,' I say. 'My habit is still dry enough. It will keep us both warm.'

He stands closely for a moment, as if welcoming my touch, but then he turns away.

'If it means so much to you,' I say, in the most gentle tone I can manage, 'I promise not to gaze upon you.'

But of course I do. I cannot help myself. The boy's form is so fine that even the touch of his habit between my fingers excites me. And, as I lift the cloth up and over his legs, his hips, his behind, I cannot but feast on his beauteous perfection.

As I use the driest part of my own habit to wipe him down, he offers no resistance. Soon, with his back, buttocks and legs now clear of moisture, I gloss my fingers over his bare shoulders. More and more, I feel a need to face him, to embrace him. But, more and more, any pressure I place on his shoulder meets with firm resistance.

'Please, Eamon,' I say. 'Please. I can sense you are still cold. Let me dry you. And there is room, as I have said, inside my habit for us both.'

'There may be,' says Eamon. 'But I fear you will not desire such intimacy when you discover my secret.'

'What secret is that?' I say. 'Surely there can be no secrets between us now.'

'No?' he says. 'There may be one at least.'

And he turns.

EAMON'S TRUTH
REVEALED

I say he, because until this moment, Eamon has been to me, is still, a brother, albeit the most loving and cherished of brothers. But in his turning, he comes to reveal ...

Perhaps I should have realised that my attraction to Eamon, a brother monk, was all along unnatural. Perhaps I should have sensed the sin in it more acutely. Do I, in this moment, feel forgiven? I am not sure. But even though I am transported by the Aphroditic beauty that now stands before me, I can do nothing else but stagger back. I feel far more complex and confusing emotions thrust upon me.

'You are disgusted?' she says.

'No ... no,' I stutter. 'But how ... How did you manage? For so long? And why? Surely you must have realised what might have happened if Father Melachlin or any of the others had discovered.'

'I have been careful,' she says.

I sense her need to cover herself again and, rather than have her don her wet habit, I strip off my own and pass it over. Given the events of the previous night, I am unashamed, and, thankfully, drained of any excitation.

'Come,' I say. 'And sit. If you have a mind to, please tell me your story.'

We sit and I grab some heather to cover myself.

'To begin with,' I say. 'What is your name? Your real name?'

'My name is Niamh,' she says. 'But, in truth, I have not answered to it for so long I had almost forgotten it.'

'And your family?' I say. 'Clearly you are not the second son of the second son of a king.'

'Clearly not,' says Niamh. 'But claiming that heritage was a good way of hiding from questions. And of explaining how I have come to be so educated.'

'And the truth?' I ask. 'Are you indeed royalty? A princess out for adventure?'

'Sadly, no,' she says. 'I am just the bastard daughter of a wilful nun. My mother was a sister in the convent at Killeaney.'

'So you—'

'Yes,' she says. 'I was raised in the convent. It is there, through my mother, that I had access to books and learning.'

'And your father?' I ask. 'Do you know—'

'No, not for sure,' says Niamh. 'But I have heard it told that he was an abbot from the nearby monastery.'

I gasp.

'You mean ... Father Melachlin?' I say. 'Does he know? Has he been told?'

'No, not to my knowledge,' says Niamh. 'And I would prefer it remained so. For as long as it might last, posing as a boy has allowed me to continue my study of the scriptures. As a woman, unless I was to return to the cloistered life of a nun, such study would be impossible.'

It feels as if a giant weight has fallen between us, both consequential yet somehow liberating. We are changed people. Even the child's play of the night before now seems cheap and tawdry.

'I am sorry,' I say. 'For last night. I should not have let you ...'

'It was not all your doing,' she says. 'I wanted to. If you remember, it was I who made the approach. You may find it strange, Niall, but my behaviour, my actions, although impulsive as they were, were a true expression of my feelings.'

I lower my eyes and, try as I might to resist, I find myself pressing against the heather.

'So, is it time?' Niamh continues. 'Dare we risk the mist? Dare we try to reach Cruinn and his people with a warning, before the monster brings them harm?'

I look outside. The mist, though lifting, is still thick.

'No, not yet,' I say. 'I think, for now, we are stuck fast. At least until the mist clears some more. As I say, not fifty yards into that soup would see us lost for sure. But this will give your habit a little more time to dry and your foot a little more time to heal.'

'Then if it is all the same to you,' says Niamh, with a

smile. 'I think perhaps we should entertain a risk of another sort.'

She surprises me by rising to her knees and pulling my habit back over her shoulders. Then she casts it away, revealing to me, for the first time in close proximity, the full length of her torso. I have seen the female body this close before, I have four sisters, but I have seen none such as this. Her breasts, though small, are well-rounded and her mound is covered in a soft coating of hair.

She looks at me, brazenly, but with the deepest sincerity.

'Are you sure?' I ask.

'No, not at all,' she says. 'But I am sure it will pass the time.'

I feel myself aquiver, a common feeling in recent days.

'Where do we start?' I ask. 'I am very much a novice here.'

'As am I,' she says. 'A kiss, I think. We should start with a kiss.'

But neither of us moves. It is as if each is waiting for the other to begin.

It is becoming, I decide, for the man to start proceedings. So I lean forward and, wrapping my hand gently behind her head, I draw her lips to mine. They are dry, and I can feel the cracks brought on by many days in the sun. But the contact is enough to bring a shiver through my body. I can feel her breath on mine and, surprisingly, can taste her breakfast snails on my tongue.

We embrace, deeper, and, as if it knows the way, I feel my body taking over. It needs no prompting, no lessons in love. My lips move towards her cheek, then her neck, and my hand, without proper invitation, finds its way to her breast. I fondle, unsure what, if any, pressure I should apply. All I can tell is that her teat is high and hard, a sign, I hope, that I am doing no wrong.

'Come,' she says. 'Let us lie down.' And once again it is Niamh who takes the lead. She takes my hand and we lay on the heather, in time for the morning sun to break through the mist and wash us with its light. Once again, I take in the beauty that is the female form. My hand runs slowly over her shoulder and along her flank until it reaches her hip. Almost without thought, I find myself toying with the hairs of her mound.

'How far should we ...?' I ask. 'I mean, should we ...?'

'Probably not,' she says. 'We might take some precautions, but despite all our best efforts, I fear I might fall with child. As much joy as such an act might bring, I feel we should err on the side of caution.'

'But what, then?' I say. 'What can we ...?'

'Perhaps,' she says. An expression crosses her face, a look of mischief I have not seen before. She rolls onto her back and runs her own hand across her groin.

'Perhaps you might ...' she says. 'Would you dare? The act I performed for you last night. I would welcome your performing a similar act for me now.'

I hesitate, until she spreads her legs wide in an uncommon welcome.

'Well?'

I could speak of what comes next, divulge the act I perform, but I am gallant enough to keep our secret. It is enough to say that as her body begins to tremble and I feel her pulling tightly on my hair, I know I have succeeded in bringing her some pleasure. I join her along the full length of our bed and wipe the sweat from her brow. We do not speak. I watch her until she relaxes and her breathing returns to normal.

I find myself deep in thought. Her beauty, I realise, will become unattainable again if we return to our brothers. The only way we might continue this connection, sinful as it is, is for us to venture off on our own. It would bring many risks, I think, but many rewards also.

'Do you think,' I ask, 'we might continue on our own path together? And not rejoin Father Melachlin and the others? It will be difficult, but I wonder if we might create a life for ourselves in the interior of this land. I am sure we can learn how to hunt and fish, and there are plenty of resources with which people can build a shelter.'

'You care for me that much?' says Niamh. 'And you have no fear of any wandering Picts?'

I think, for a moment too long.

'No,' she says. 'It is a poor idea. The truth be told, as much as my heart is yours, my mind is still drawn to the libraries of Killeaney. I feel I must return there someday soon. And besides. The mist has now cleared and the sky is blue. Even with my injured foot, I think we must try to reach the village of Cruinn and his friends in time to warn them of the beast's approach.'

Hard as it is to accept, I know what she says is true. It would be foolish, nay, irresponsible and cowardly, to leave our fellows to their fate. The truth is, we have no choice. We must return to Cruinn and his village and warn them of their impending doom.

Niamh stands, her body as naked as any Greek statue, and reaches for our habits. In one motion, she pulls her own habit over her head and is clothed again, denying my eyes any sight of her beauty. She tosses my habit into my lap.

'Hurry. Dress,' she says. 'We should not waste time.'

'I agree,' I say. 'But before we go. I still worry about your blistered foot. Your walking yesterday has torn the linen and scattered the chamomile Cruinn used as a medicant. I believe we should wash and dress your wounds again before we leave.'

'What you say makes sense,' says Niamh, 'but I feel any chamomile and fresh linen will be hard to find nearby.'

'Perhaps so,' I say, pulling on my habit. 'What we do now will only be a temporary fix. But we can get Cruinn to dress it again when we return to the village. Now sit down and offer me your foot.'

For a moment, even though we have just engaged in all manner of delight, the renewed touch of her skin brings more unexpected pleasure. I run my hand slowly over her calf and ankle before reaching her foot, then, taking all the care that I can, I unroll the dirty linen and peel away the chamomile leaves from her wounds. The chamomile and honey and lemon have, I see, done their work. Although the blisters are still visible, they are now smaller in size and much less fierce.

'I will be back in a moment,' I say.

I stand and take the linen down to the loch's edge and rinse it. Although it is useless now as a dressing, I know I can use it to wash the wounds. I let the water soak it several times before I squeeze it tightly and return to Niamh.

'Hold still,' I say. 'This might be uncomfortable.'

I see her wince as I dab the worst of the sores.

'It will not take long,' I continue. 'But I feel it is important to get them clean.'

It takes barely a moment and the sole of Niamh's left foot is free of dirt and grime. The skin is white and soft, wrinkled, as if she had recently bathed, and the half a dozen blisters are shrunken and no longer inflamed.

'We have no chamomile,' I say. 'But there is plenty of heather growing wild here. I am sure it will work as a temporary measure.'

'And the dressing?' says Niamh. 'The linen is useless.'

'I know,' I say.

I take my habit and, biting hard into the hem, I tear a strip several inches wide around the circumference of the garment. Soon, with the softest heather flowers applied, I have bound the foot securely. And, although it may be a little too tight for comfort, I manage to fit her sandal. A solid substance under her foot, I think, will protect the dressing from any dirt or stones it might encounter.

'Are you able to stand?' I ask.

'With some help,' she says. 'Give me your arm. And pass me my staff.'

I help her to her feet and she hobbles toward the cave's entrance.

'I will manage,' she says. 'And I am sure that when we reach the flat surface near the shore, I will find the going easier.'

WE RETURN TO THE VILLAGE

S o we begin our return to the village, along the shore of the loch and over the soft grassy field that flanks it. And, as she has promised, Niamh makes strong and steady progress. I know she is in pain, but, from the stern expression on her face, I cannot tell how much.

'We have made progress already,' I say. 'We have come some four hundred yards in the matter of minutes.'

'And the village,' says Niamh. 'It looks like we may be closer than we thought. I can see smoke. It appears as if last night's pyres are still burning.'

'So it seems,' I say.

I can see plumes of grey smoke rising in the distance.

'I am surprised,' I say. 'I would have expected their celebrations to be concluded by now. Be still for a moment. Can you hear their carousing? Or have they left the pyres to burn and are now all sleeping off their inebriation?'

We hush ... and listen. What we hear is not a people deep in slumber, but a place wild with activity. Shouting, cries, the din of raucous behaviour, all reach our ears.

'I am surprised,' says Niamh. 'I would have thought that after last night's ceremony, they might all be grumbling and holding their heads low.'

'I would have thought so, too,' I say. 'But whatever their state of mind, it seems they are ill prepared for the monster, should it arrive. Come. If you can, let us hurry our pace. I am not sure they will listen, but if we are able, we must give them all the warning we can.'

We cross the grassy area, wade through some weeds and shallow, swampy water, then squeeze our way past another rocky outcrop. All that remains, I think, is a gentle hill and an easy decline to the village below.

Our journey has only a few hundred yards to go. But there is something wrong. I sense it. The smoke the village offers is far more than the leftovers of a few funeral pyres and, this close, the shouting and cries are more immediate. They are in some cases bloodcurdling, sounds made in fear or terror rather than joy or celebration. I can tell that Niamh, too, is hesitant. The expression on her face, the way her nails bite into my arm, tell me she too has doubts.

'What shall we do?' she asks.

'I am not sure,' I say. 'I think there may be danger if we approach the village head on. Something dire has clearly happened there. I suggest we scale that hill to the south. Upon its summit, I feel we may find a vantage point from which to reconnoiter. Can you manage the incline?'

'For sure,' says Niamh. 'The pain in my foot is constant, but I can endure.'

'It is best,' I say, 'if we remain unseen. Whatever is happening in the village, I am certain there is nothing to be gained by revealing ourselves.'

'I agree,' says Niamh. She begins her shuffle away, towards the southern slope. My precautions, I think, may still be unwarranted, but nevertheless, I keep low and follow.

Despite Niamh's occasional need to pause, it is not long before we reach the foot of the hill. It will not be difficult, I decide, for me to climb, to crawl if necessary, and peer over the rise at the village below. In moments, I am sure, I will understand exactly the state of play inside the village.

'Wait here,' I say. 'I will let you know if it is safe to follow.'

'I will do no such thing,' says Niamh. 'I have not lived my life thus far shying away from danger. I will not start now.'

'Fine,' I say. 'I will not argue. But keep low. If there is danger to be had, then it is not ideal that we bring it upon ourselves.'

THE NORSEMEN AT WORK

S himmying on elbows and knees, we creep towards the rise, all the time listening to the cries and wails from the village below and watching the pillars of now black smoke rising high into the sky. We stop at the summit and, careful not to be seen, we peer over. But what we find is not the consequence of a night of carousing. It is, to the astonishment of both our gentle souls, a sign of Hell on Earth. Every hut in the village is ablaze. Awash with blood, its warriors lay strewn in various stages of ruin. Carnage abounds. And in the distance, on the edge of the loch, through the smoke, we can see the partial form of the beast, its mighty, menacing head held high above ...

But no. At a second look, we can tell. This is no form of beast at all. The beast's head, that thing the image of which had terrified us at our cave, is but the figurehead of a ship. It is a ship the size of which I have never seen before. It is difficult to tell through the smoke, but I would gauge that the ship must be sixty or seventy feet long, even more, and fifteen or twenty feet wide at its girth. And, to our horror, those women of the village not yet dead or dying are being led screaming on board, some bound, some at the edge of a sword, by the most fearsome set of warriors we could imagine. If ever we considered the Picts to be wild, then these men are ten times worse. They are perhaps the most savage creatures we have ever encountered. All are tall and muscular, far beyond the size of ordinary men, and each of those not shaven-clean grows his hair and his beard down to his waist and beyond. Each is armoured with a polished helmet, a colourful shield and a glistening sword.

I open my mouth to whisper, but no words come.

'They are Norsemen,' says Niamh. 'I have heard of their raids further south and, from time to time, even upon the villages of Hibernia. They are known for their attacks on monasteries. They are Godless, or at least they worship a set of their own pagan gods unlike anything else we have encountered. And in stripping the monasteries of their gold and jewels, they will happily torture and slay any monks they find, or lead them to be sold as slaves in far off lands.'

'And is that,' I say, 'their intention with the women below?'

'No doubt,' says Niamh. 'They will be taken to Constantinople to be sold as harem slaves or, perhaps worse, be taken as chattels to the Norsemen's homeland itself.'

'We can be thankful, then,' I say, 'that we are here

and not there. That we chose to leave the village last night and not indulge in their festivities.'

The slaughter and mayhem continues, until eventually the din subsides and all that remains is sobbing and the sight of Norsemen putting the wounded and already half-dead to the sword.

'I can watch no more of this,' says Niamh, as she turns away. She lays on her back and, although I do not think she is crying, she covers her eyes.

While Niamh keeps her back to the destruction below, I remain vigilant, in the ever-decreasing hope that some of the villagers, children even, might survive. But this seems unlikely. Before long, all who have not been slaughtered by the Norsemen have been herded onto their vessel. Then, with the efforts of half a dozen of their burliest warriors, the ship is pushed off the shore and back into the water. The men hustle on board and, with some subtle oar work, they direct the ship into the centre and deepest part of the loch.

'They are leaving,' I say. 'Perhaps we, too, should make time. In all likelihood, these Norsemen will continue up the loch now, towards the village of Domelch and her people, towards Father Melachlin and our brothers. If possible, we must arrive there first, armed with all the knowledge of these people we might carry.'

'I agree,' says Niamh, now returning her gaze towards the village. 'But, first, I hope a few at least might have survived down there. I think we should take a moment and search for them.'

I have my doubts, but I cannot deny her wisdom. I help her to her feet and, negotiating the summit of the hill, we descend towards the village below.

'But as important as this task is,' I say, 'I feel we should not tarry. Even assuming the Norsemen stop and make camp overnight, we will find it difficult to reach the village before them.'

'We must do what we must do,' says Niamh. 'Come, let us look among these bodies for any sign of life.'

WE SEARCH THE VILLAGE

We reach the edge of the village and, stepping over body after body, we wade through the blood and entrails of folk with whom, in all likelihood, we might once have shared a meal. But hardly any of the bodies, I note, are complete. Some are missing arms, some legs. And a good many are headless. If I had any doubts, I now take this as certain confirmation that it is the ship of these Norsemen, rather than some unlikely beast, that has been haunting the shores of the loch. And it strikes me, too. None of these bodies, it seems, will be given a grand passage to the afterlife such as we have witnessed so far. They will become food for the crows already gathering nearby. And there is nothing we can do, I realise, to protect them from this assault.

'Hello?' I call, well aware that, even if they have survived, none of the villagers are likely to understand my words. But I hope the announcement, at least, might draw someone back from the gates of death. Niamh, too, calls out, drawing as close as she can to the burning huts and peering inside.

We have searched a good half of the village when my patience begins to thin.

'We should go,' I say. 'This exercise is pointless. This is nothing more than a meal for the dogs and crows.'

'Stay,' says Niamh. 'I have not yet given up hope. There must be at least one who has escaped the blade of a Norseman, one who has hidden in an unspoiled hut or under an upturned cart.'

It is as if we are traipsing through Hades itself. But finally, when we have almost reached our fill of the ghostlike glares of the dead, we hear the unmistakable cries of life. They come from amid a pile of bodies near the entrance to a hut. Niamh is first to reach them. She pulls away at the bodies, first one and then another, until, at the bottom, as I look over her shoulder, she reaches the pained, distressed form of Cruinn's wife, Eithni. The woman is covered in blood, issuing from a deep wound in her side. One of her legs, too, her thigh, has been cut. Although she lives, the Norsemen have shown her no mercy.

'Hurry,' says Niamh. 'Her wounds need binding.'

I look around. With no complaints from the dead and plenty of fabric to steal, it is not long before her injuries are bound. But we have done nothing to ease her pain and, already, she shows signs of a fever.

'What do we do?' I say. 'We cannot leave her here. If we do, she will surely die. Yet neither can we stay with her. Not unless we forego the warning of Father Melachlin and our brothers.'

'Which we cannot do,' says Niamh. 'We need to build something. A stretcher of sorts. In that way we can carry her. She is small and light. I am sure, with some effort, we might manage.'

Niamh, I can tell, is already thinking ahead. She has reached for two idle spears and a length of cloth. Showing no fear, she then strips a few of the dead of their knives, their belts and the strips of leather they wear around their necks. It is not hard to understand her plan.

'I can see what you hope to achieve,' I say. 'But I am not sure we can manage. It must be thirty miles or more to the other village. With your damaged foot, it will be an arduous enough task for you. To expect you to help carry this woman—'

Niamh looks at her foot. It is almost as if, for a time, she has forgotten her injury.

'I—' she begins.

Then, out of nowhere, we hear something else. It is not the cries of the woman, the barking of dogs or the shouts and screams of the Norsemen. It is a ringing, not unlike that of the monastery bells back in Killeaney.

'Where?' I ask.

'Be quiet,' says Niamh. 'It is not loud, but it is close.'

We look around. My eyes see it first. In the centre of the clearing between the huts, next to the fire that once warmed our soup, lies the upturned cauldron that held it.

'Do you think ...?' I ask.

'It is possible,' says Niamh. 'But take care. We have no idea what the pot hides.'

She signals towards the sword of one of the fallen Picts.

'It is best you arm yourself,' she says.

I have qualms, but I pick up the sword and we approach. I hit the pot with the hilt and it sounds in a sure and steady ring. Then, in a moment, another ring answers.

'There is something or someone inside,' I say to Niamh. 'Here, hold the sword while I turn it.'

'Take care,' she replies. 'It may be a trap.'

I reach for the rim of the cauldron and prepare to lift. It is heavy, but, in an instant, I feel some assistance from inside. The cauldron rolls, with a loud clang, to reveal ... I find it hard to understand exactly how he has managed, but the former Father Cillian has squeezed himself inside. With little more room left for air, he has huddled into a ball and filled the pot.

Now freed of his lair, he stands and stretches.

'I thank you,' he says. 'For a while, I thought I might be stuck. I thought I might die with the smell of my own farts on my nostrils. Did you see them? They came like marauders, out of nowhere, showing no mercy to any that stood in their way. I had only just enough time to tip the pot and climb inside.'

'And your wife?' says Niamh, in a low tone. 'You gave her no thought? You would have forgotten her?'

The gruffness in her voice, I understand, is partly for my benefit, a reminder to me that she has now returned to her guise as Brother Eamon.

'Did you not consider her safety?' she continues. 'Or was your sole concern the saving of your own skin?'

'I asked the Lord to protect her,' says Cruinn. 'And I see her there. It seems as if He has answered my prayer.'

'Hardly so,' says Niamh. 'Had we not come along, she would have died a slow and painful death. You, too, might have cooked inside your pot.'

'But, in any case, all is well, now,' says Cruinn. 'For the four of us, at least. I feel that for these dead villagers that lie around us, however, there is nothing we can do. They must lie unattended and uncared for. It is their fate, sadly, to spend their afterlife stuck on the outskirts of paradise. Come now, let us head inland. We might find some security there should the barbarians return.'

'No,' says Niamh, in as firm a voice as I have heard. 'You can leave in any direction you choose, but we must return and warn our brothers. And take heed. Eithni's injuries will require all the care we can manage.'

The old man rubs his chin and then nods.

'Fine, then,' he says. 'If we must, we shall accompany you. As it is said, one can die only once. I may as well die on the blade of some angry Norseman. Knowing my luck, if we were to head inland, I would most likely meet an excruciating end by eating some hemlock root or perhaps a poisonous toadstool. I have been pampered for so long here in this village, have had my every need attended to, I can no longer tell what is safe and what is not.'

'Good,' says Niamh. 'Now go. Look around and see if you can find anything that might help in tending Eithni's wounds. And my own, while you are at it ... And Niall. Come and help me add the finishing touches to this stretcher.'

Cruinn wanders away and I assist Niamh in binding the fabric to the spears.

'I had a thought,' she says, 'that he would have been happier to see her taken by the Norseman. Or, even worse, I doubt he would have cast a tear were he to have found her corpse when he finally escaped from his cast iron tomb.'

She scoffs.

'I feel,' she continues, 'that his many years with these people have taken him far from the spirit of the Lord. Whatever he was to begin with, he has now become little more than a gluttonous, selfish old man. Perhaps we might be better served by leaving him behind, leaving him to his own devices.'

'In other circumstances, that might be an option,' I say. 'But remember. We cannot leave Eithni, either alone or in the care of Cruinn. And, like it or not, with your foot still so impaired, we might welcome some assistance in carrying her. Although she is light, so are you. Cruinn is a big man and will carry her weight easily.'

'Your words are true,' says Niamh. 'I am sure,

however, that he will resist doing any scrap of work. We will have to force him into taking up his part of the load.'

She is correct. The old man is full of excuses and it is only when we threaten to abandon him that he agrees to pull his weight.

WE FOLLOW THE NORSEMEN

With Eithni's wounds tended and Niamh's foot re-dressed, we continue on. And with me in front and Cruinn at the rear of the stretcher, we follow the loch again, heading westward, all the time on the lookout for the Norsemen's ship. Niamh walks alongside me, troubled by her foot but aided by the staff she still carries. Even so, every half an hour or so we stop, to allow her and Cruinn some time to rest. Niamh is mostly silent, taking time on occasion to drink or to wash her face, while the old man moans and complains about the pain in his back or the growing blisters on his hands.

'Perhaps,' he suggests. 'Perhaps ... You are a strong man. Were I to let my end drop to the ground, you might be able to drag the stretcher from the front. I have seen it done.'

'No,' I say strongly. 'I am not a horse. Nor am I an ox. I am not your beast of burden.'

'Then what about the boy?' he says. 'I know he is wounded. But perhaps if we were to take turns. Just twenty minutes or half an hour at a time.'

'Eithni is your wife,' I say. 'If you are not careful, I will leave you to carry her entire load. Now come. It is time to press on. And from now on, I suggest you do so in silence. If I am not mistaken, the Norsemen will not wish to spend the night onboard their vessel. They will stop and make camp onshore again before coming upon Domelch's village in the morning. At any point, we might stumble across them again. And in that case, any noise we make may be our last. You, Cruinn, they will smell a mile downwind. And it stands, of course. If we have any hope of reaching the village in time, we must skirt the Norse camp and continue our trek through the night.'

The day passes quickly and it is not long before the bright sun, sinking before us, hampers our vision. I can feel myself squinting and can see Niamh holding a hand over her eyes. It will not be long, I decide, before the sun will be so low it will be directly in our faces. It will not be long before we might step, blindly and unannounced, straight into the Norsemen's camp.

We stop for a moment and Cruinn and I drop Eithni's stretcher to the ground.

'It is time,' I say. 'We should rest for a short while before we head inland. A mile or so should be far enough. Then we might continue our journey westward without danger of stumbling into the Norsemen.'

Cruinn opens his mouth in certain complaint, but

then stops. I think he understands the sense in my strategy.

'Then let us do it quickly,' he says. 'We should make do with whatever light is left.'

So we turn southward, away from the loch, and follow a row of lonely pines until, after half an hour or so, we reach a more thickly wooded area.

'I believe this will be far enough southwards,' I say. 'I believe these woods will give us all the cover we need.'

'I agree,' says Niamh. 'And while I suspect that the underbrush may be difficult to negotiate, I believe a few needles in our feet are better than blades in our bellies.'

WE JOURNEY THROUGH
THE NIGHT

Nothing more is said. In silence, we enter the woods and resume our journey westward. The sun, now very low, peeks intermittently through the trees, providing for us a decent pointer to chase. That is, until it finally sinks below the horizon and, apart from a short-lived remnant glow, it leaves us in a murky gloom. Even that glow, after another hour, is gone and we must proceed in total darkness, in the hope that our sense of direction does not fail us and we do not suddenly come upon the Norse encampment.

But we do not, at this stage, have much to fear. All we can see are the silhouettes of the trees and our companions and all we can hear, apart from the crunch of pine cones under our feet, is the occasional howling of wolves. Then, as time passes, we can see, in the distance to our right, a brighter glow, the brightness, no doubt, of the Norsemen's fire, and we can hear, as if from the loch itself, the din that is their laughter.

'I think there is enough distance between us,' I say. 'I believe we will be safe enough if we stick close to the tree line.'

We continue on, but the line of trees brings us closer and closer to the camp. Soon the fire's light is flickering on our shoulders and we can see the actual figures of the Norsemen. Most, I suspect, are intoxicated and engaging in all manner of violence against the women they have taken. I turn my head away.

'I can only imagine the suffering of their captives,' I say.

'I would rather you didn't,' says Niamh. 'Perhaps we can pray instead that the Lord brings to them a quick and merciful end. And remember. If we are found, while some of our party may not last long, others may be left to join in the suffering.'

I hold my tongue and we continue, haunted by the distinct voice of a sole carousing Norseman.

It is easy to tell that Niamh and especially Cruinn are close to exhaustion. Eithni, it appears, has been in and out of consciousness since our journey began. On that point, I am thankful. Any unwanted sound from her might have given our position away. In any case, it is necessary that we put some distance between ourselves and the Norse camp before we stop and rest again. I urge Niamh and Cruinn to press on.

It takes us about an hour before the light of the Norsemen's fire fades behind the hillocks to our rear and we consider it safe enough to emerge from the trees.

'Perhaps not straight away,' I say. 'But soon, we

might resume our passage towards the loch. We will find the going there far easier.'

'Certainly,' says Cruinn. 'But I beg of you. Give us some more respite now. We will be of no help to your comrades if we are stone dead before we even arrive. Look at the boy there. You have exhausted him.'

I look to Niamh. For sure, she is as tired as I have seen her. She is sitting and trying, with the utmost care, to rearrange the dressing on her foot.

'Are you able to continue?' I ask her. 'Perhaps if I go on alone, I can make better time. Like one of your Greek friends, Pheidippides of Athens.'

She looks at me quizzically.

'I told you,' I laugh. 'I am not entirely ignorant.'

'Perhaps not,' says Niamh. 'But if you remember the end of the story, Pheidippides died when he completed his task. No, I do not wish for that fate to befall you.'

'Then, for a time,' I suggest. 'Perhaps I might carry you on my shoulders. It might be possible for Cruinn to do something similar with Eithni.'

'No,' says Niamh flatly. 'Please do not to treat me as a useless waif. I will manage. Only now we are clear of the Norsemen, just give me a few moments. Cruinn, too, I am sure, will welcome some rest. And, although you do not seem willing to admit it, I believe that even you need a halt to our proceedings.'

I take my scolding to heart and turn away. Cruinn, I notice, is trying to collect the night's dew from the needles of the pine cones. He uses a piece of cloth to dab the mouth of his still unconscious wife. I am surprised.

It is the first time, almost, that I have seen him show her anything like affection.

'She is very weak,' he says. 'I fear if we do not reach the village soon and get her some proper care, she will not survive.'

I find myself holding my tongue here, as well. The truth is simple, I realise. Even if, by some miracle, we are able to reach the village in time, it will be in time only to warn its inhabitants and prepare for their evacuation.

I wonder, as I watch Niamh picking at her foot, and Cruinn, tending to his wife, exactly how I managed to become responsible for such a band. Because Niamh's complaints aside, responsible is how I feel. I have, in truth, become the accidental leader of this crew. And in becoming so, I have become responsible not only for them, but for the hundred or so souls now sleeping without a care in Domelch's village.

'I guess we have time,' I say, although I sense I am the only one listening. I follow Cruinn's lead and search for the rare drop of moisture on the needles of the pine cones. There is little to be had, so I slump onto the ground beside Niamh. But it is a mistake. As soon as I land, I feel a wave of exhaustion pour over me. It is all I can do to stop myself from closing my eyes and finding sleep.

'No,' I say. 'We cannot rest. We must press on. An entire village depends on our actions this night. Niamh … I mean, Brother Eamon. Quickly. Please re-bandage your foot as best you can. And Cruinn. In less than an hour we will reach the loch again. Then, Eithni can have all the water she needs. And her chances of surviving will be that much greater the sooner we reach the village. Hurry, Cruinn. Grab the stretcher and let us depart.'

It is not without a share of grumbling and complaint, but soon we are on our way again, heading a little north of westward, towards what I hope are the loch and the Pictish village. Although we are clear of the trees and the starry night offers us some light, the brightness of the Norse fire is hidden from us now. None of us is skilled in following the sky by night and we can only hope we have not lost our way and are at any moment about to stumble across a Norse sentry or his sleeping fellows.

But the Lord, it seems, is still on our side. It takes us less than the hour predicted before we hear the waves of the loch and then see the glint of moonlight as it dances across the water.

It seems neither Niamh nor Cruinn will listen to me now. Niamh is quick to follow my example by tearing a strip from the bottom of her habit. Soaking it in the cold water of the loch, she begins to clean her bloodied foot. Cruinn uses his hands as a cup and brings replenishment to Eithni. I neither complain nor resist. I realise it is pointless to do so. They are far too absorbed in what have become essential tasks. Also, according to my most basic calculations, we still have several hours of night left and only a few more miles remain between us and the village.

The sole of her foot now clean of dried blood and

dirt, Niamh tears yet another strip from her habit and binds it again. But with the garment now shortened, her legs are in open view. Try as I might to avoid it, the sight of them arouses me. I can but wonder if we will ever experience again the intimacy we shared in the cave.

But enough of that thinking for now. It does me no good to journey off on flights of fancy or dreams of what might be. I wait until I see Niamh's foot well-bandaged and some resolve return to the old man's eyes.

'Come then,' I say, taking hold of the stretcher once again. 'Let us press on. If I am not mistaken, our next stop will be the village itself.'

There is no argument now. Niamh uses her staff to get to her feet and Cruinn takes the other end of the stretcher. We march, or walk, or hobble, until the night is done and the light of the dawning sun casts long shadows before us. Not much more time passes before we stand high on a bluff looking down on the village below.

DOMELCH'S VILLAGE

As I suspect, the villagers are deep in slumber. I can see wisps of smoke from their all-night fires and the bodies of my brethren as they lie sleeping around the largest of the fires. I am thankful, both to have reached the village and to see my brothers once again. I am thankful, most of all, that there is no sign of the Norse ship and its evil crew.

'Come,' I say. 'Let us not delay. We do not know for sure how much time we have before the beasts are upon us.'

To the barking of dogs and the growling of once-dozing guards, we enter the camp. Niamh bangs on a kettle with her staff.

'Awake! Awake!' she cries and, if our language is not enough to alert them, Cruinn joins in, crying something in the Pictish tongue. The Picts are slow to emerge from their huts, but my brethren are quick to awaken. Rising, they make their way towards us. Several, good souls that they are, take Eithni from our hands and tend to her wounds.

'Brother Niall,' says Father Mechalin. 'Why all this distress? And who are these people? And why have you neglected the mission I sent you on?'

'All will be explained, Father,' I say. 'But first. We must gather everyone and prepare to leave the village. There is a menace coming from further down the loch, the likes of which you cannot imagine.'

'Not the fabled monster?' the Father laughs.

If I am not mistaken, he offers me a wink.

'Remember, Niall,' he continues. 'We need have no fear of that thing. I have long since put its danger to bed. We have not seen hide nor hair of it since you left.'

'No, Father,' says Niamh, tugging at his habit and speaking with all the force and conviction she can muster. 'It is something far, far worse. The beast these people feared is nothing other than the figurehead on the bow of a Norse ship. And if we are not mistaken, these Norsemen will be with us shortly, set on plunder and destruction.'

But all Father Melachlin does is glower.

'Hush, Brother Eamon,' he says, brushing her away. 'And settle yourself. For the smallest and youngest of our brethren, you seem to have grown a mighty big voice in a very short length of time.'

'I hate to admit it,' says Cruinn. 'But what the boy says is true.'

Father Melachlin looks Cruinn up and down, as if examining something rank and distasteful.

'And who, pray tell, are you?' he says. 'Or what are you? You wear the garb of the heathen, but I see you have the cross of our Lord hanging about your neck.'

'I am Father Cillian,' says Cruinn. 'Of Cloher. I have been in this land a little longer than I anticipated. I have become somewhat used to their ways.'

'You are a disgrace,' says Father Melachlin. 'To the Church and to the Lord.'

Cruinn merely grins, as if the Father's words do not matter. He finds a home among the now gathering Picts.

'And this?' says Father Melachlin, signalling towards Eithni's supine form. 'Please do not confirm for me what I already suspect.'

'Yes, indeed,' says Cruinn. 'She is my wife. She has been so for the last dozen years past.'

'Enough, please,' I say. 'There will be enough time later for you to continue your squabbling. We cannot tarry. We must do everything in our power to convince the Picts to leave this village and seek the safety of the inland forests.'

'Piffle,' says Father Mechalin. 'These Norsemen you describe cannot be so dangerous that we cannot parley with them. I will happily lead the way. It took me but an act of showmanship and some faith in the Lord to bring these heathen into His flock. I will bring these Norsemen into the fold in the same way.'

I open my mouth, but realise the pointlessness of arguing. Any success, I decide, will not be achieved by negotiating with this cantankerous old man.

'Come, Brother Eamon,' I say. 'Let us explain to our

brethren the dire straits we are in. Cruinn, or perhaps I should say Father Cillian ... It might be best if you explain our situation to the villagers. That woman there ... her name is Domelch ... She holds some kind of leadership role among her people.'

'I will do as you suggest,' says Cruinn. 'I am as well being of some use before exhaustion runs me through.'

Niamh and I take a few steps away and, to my surprise, most of our brethren follow, keen to hear our report. We must appear atrocious to them, I think, hardly the orderly travellers who left them just a few days past.

'Brothers, we must abandon this village,' says Niamh. 'It will not be long before a mighty ship filled with the most vicious warriors imaginable comes sailing up the loch. I have no doubts they will destroy this village as they did the last. They will kill all the men and take all the women as their own. And have no doubts. The youngest and softest of you. They will take you like women, too, before sending you off to Jesus.'

I see a few of our brethren shake, which is all the response we might have hoped for. Whatever the final response of Father Melachlin, I am now confident most of our brothers will join us in our flight.

'But where shall we go?' asks Brother Feargus. 'Where can we go where these Norsemen will not pursue?'

'To the south,' I say. 'We might, in the short term, hide in those hills and, if necessary, we might flee into the woods beyond.'

'And what? We would just abandon the good Father?' says Brother Aengus. 'That seems to me an act of little faith. And what of the Picts who decide to stay? Those whom Father Melachlin has managed to baptise? Can we in all faith just leave them to their fate?'

'We need not be so hasty in our decisions, Aengus,' says Niamh. 'Let us learn, for starters, what they plan to do. For all we know, they might decide to take to the woods along with us.'

I turn towards Cruinn, who is deep in conversation with Domelch and a few of her followers. But there is little satisfaction in his expression. It seems the decision here has also been made. The Picts, their warriors at least, will stay and confront the Norsemen.

'This woman, Domelch,' says Cruinn. 'She says it is not within the spirit of her people to flee from a fight. Anyone, any man or woman who can bear arms and is willing to do so, can stand and fight for the glory of the tribe.'

'Or die for the glory of the tribe?' I say.

'Probably so,' says Cruinn. 'They may be a brave people, but I never said they were a sensible one.'

'And what about the children?' I ask. 'And the old and infirm? Will they be left to be slaughtered when the search for glory is over?'

Cruinn says something to Domelch, then the Picts exchange some words.

'She wants to know,' says Cruinn. 'Will you and your brethren stand neither arm-in-arm on the water's edge with your Father Mechalin nor behind the barricades the Picts manage to prepare?'

'No, we will not,' I say. 'We have seen these Norsemen in action. They are merciless and unstoppable. I believe there is little point in throwing ourselves at their feet.'

'Then you should flee with the children and old women, she says,' says Cruinn. 'She says you are a coward, and about as useful as the dog shit on the sole of her shoe.'

I look hard at Niamh. We both feel, for a moment, an uncomfortable rush of shame. But it passes quickly. We are both beyond any normal levels of fear and fatigue. And I hope that for her, as well as for me, life has become far too rich and beautiful to give it up so easily.

THE END COMES QUICKLY

There are more than twenty children and perhaps a dozen or so ancients. While our brother monks shepherd them into a line, Niamh and I return to Father Melachlin and Domelch, in the hope a last ditch plea might be successful. But Father Melachlin will have none of it, and Domelch and her people are already piling every obstacle they can at the front of the village. Their main defence, their sole barriers against the horde of Norsemen, will be three upturned carts.

'The Norsemen will be inside the village in seconds,' I say to Niamh. 'The position of the villagers is hopeless.'

'I agree,' she says. 'But what of Cruinn ... and Eithni? As troublesome as the old man is, surely we are not leaving him behind?'

'Unlikely,' I say. 'I am sure he will come running, or waddling, shortly.'

Sure enough, as two of our brethren carry Eithni towards us, Father Cillian joins them.

'I was beginning to wonder, Cruinn,' I say. 'I thought you may have found the Lord again. Enough, at least, to join Father Melachlin in his final ministry.'

'Unlikely,' he says. 'I have heard it said. The Lord helps those who help themselves. I believe this is one of those times.'

Any decisions have now been made and we are split into two camps, those who will stay and those who will go. Father Melachlin and two of our brethren stand praying, knee deep in the loch's cool water. A collection of perhaps forty or fifty men and women, some I hesitate to call warriors, collect what weapons or tools they can. That leaves the young and old, Cruinn and Eithni, and the eight of our brethren who have chosen to accompany us. With a parting glance towards Father Melachlin, Niamh and I lead this troop away and up the rise that marks the southern boundary of the village.

'How far do we need to go?' asks Niamh.

'I suggest we push them until they can go no more,' I say. 'But I plan to wait beyond the hill. I need to know what transpires, in case our evacuation has been for naught.'

'Then I shall stay with you,' says Niamh. 'Our brethren and Father Cillian can take perfect care of the villagers. And you might need someone to prompt you if your stubbornness endangers you.'

The children cry for their parents and the old people cry for their breakfasts, but there is no time to indulge them. The Norsemen may appear at any time and if we are sighted, that will be the end of us. The elderly will be put to the sword and the children will be but stock for sale in the Levant. So we hurry them over the ridge at the top of the hill and into the valley below. Soon they are out of sight of the village and, thankfully, out of earshot of what may become their parents', or children's, dying screams.

'Please, Cruinn ' I say, 'Please, find your faith and spirit once again. Be as Moses for us and lead these people to safety. If you continue for about half a mile, I suspect you will come to a wooded area. I doubt the Norsemen will bother to explore that far. Wait there for us if you will.'

'But what about you?' he says. 'You are not coming with us?'

'No, not for now,' I say. 'But soon, perhaps. Brother Eamon and I need to stay and find out what unfolds below. But whatever happens, wait. We will join you shortly.'

Cruinn and the best of our brethren act as sheepdogs, coaxing and pushing the villagers away from us and towards the woods. Soon, they are but small marks in a mantle of green and Niamh and I can turn our attention to the village.

'If the Norsemen do not come,' says Niamh, 'we will not be popular.'

'Perhaps not,' I say. 'But I would rather face the ire of Domelch and Father Melachlin than the fury of the Norse. At least then there might be some escape.'

'True,' says Niamh. 'But hush. Let us watch. And listen for the sound of their oars. We might easily hear them before we see them.'

I do as she suggests, and we lie there, watching and listening. True to Niamh's word, only minutes go by before we hear the heaving of oars and see the great sail of the Norse ship come into view. And then, as the ship shifts its direction from the centre of the loch towards the shore and the village, we hear the cheers of the Norsemen and the clatter of swords upon shields. Both Niamh and I are terrified. I can only imagine the fear running through the veins of Domelch and her people.

It happens quickly. First, I hear Father Melachlin, Brother Aengus and Brother Conall shouting Latin words and see them waving crosses in the air. Then, as the Norsemen hit the shore, Father Melachlin steps forward to greet them, only to be split in two by a heathen axe. I look to Niamh for a reaction, but her cold face offers none. Neither Aengus nor Conall lasts much longer. There is no time for any final prayer to come from their lips before they are run through by the Norsemen's blades. Their bodies hit the water and the loch runs red with their blood.

I expect the Norsemen, not quick on strategy, to rush the Pictish defences. But they do not. As Pictish arrows begin to fall, the Norsemen form their own version of the Roman testudo and begin pushing forward. Soon, with very few casualties, they reach the carts the Picts have used as their wall and begin clambering over. The Pictish line, as I suspected, does not last long. In moments, men and women in loincloths but not much more drop their weapons and flee from the axes and blades of the burly Norsemen. And, one after another, each of these men and women is brought down with a scream and a gush of blood. It is not a battle, but a massacre, a rout. No song for the ages is created here.

The last of the Picts to fall is Domelch herself. Surrounded by a ring of Norse warriors, for a moment I imagine her captured and carried off to be the plaything of one of their chieftains or perhaps a Persian king. But she does not let this happen. As the Norsemen draw closer, she falls to her knees and, with a mighty heave, leans into her own sword. Although the Norsemen laugh and kick at her fallen body, and I am aware that the taking of one's own life is against God's law, I cannot help but consider. Domelch's act is, I think, among the bravest I have ever seen.

OUR FINAL FLIGHT

The Norsemen, this time, do not bother with prisoners. It seems that the first village has supplied them with trophies enough. So they spend the next short while stabbing at squirming bodies, hewing heads and setting fire to both bodies and huts. It is not long before the stench of death reaches my nostrils.

Niamh, too, scrunches her face.

'There seems little point,' she says, 'in us staying here. It seems the Norsemen might stay a while to celebrate their victory. And even if they were to leave, there is nothing we can do for these fallen souls.'

'And Father Melachlin?' I say. 'And Aengus? Conall? Do they not deserve Christian burials?'

'Deserve, yes,' says Niall. 'But I am afraid in this case, the Lord must provide for them.'

Her voice drops away.

'No, I am sorry,' she continues. 'There is nothing we

can do. I believe our next task must be to rejoin Cruinn, our dear brethren and what is now the future of the village.'

It is hard to put the dead behind us, to forget the violence and carnage we have just seen, but I find, as she takes my hand and leads me forward, that it is Niamh who gives me strength to go on.

'And now?' I ask. 'What shall we do? Our mission, it seems, is in ruins. Any Picts Father Melachlin managed to baptise are now mostly dead. And any village along the loch must be easy pickings for the Norsemen. I doubt, if we remain in this area, that we have seen the last of them.'

'What you say is true,' says Niamh. 'As far as these Norsemen are concerned, I fear this may be just the first of their invasions.'

'And us?' I say. 'Hold for a moment. I need to ask. What is to become of us? Do we rejoin our brethren, maintaining this charade that you are still Brother Eamon? Or do we reveal to them your true nature? Or should we take a new path by ourselves? Should we go off alone towards a new life together? I know that I, for one, will not be content to live the life of a celibate monk with or without you by my side.'

Niamh smiles and strokes my cheek with her fingers.

'Nor will I,' she says, 'But as much as we might like to, for the moment we cannot think just of ourselves. I have no issue, in time, with revealing my true sex to our brethren, but for now the two of us must be strong. We must act as parents to the remaining villagers. If possible, we must find them a home with others of their kind.'

Her words ring true. With the sun now rising higher in the sky, we head towards the woods. As hoped for, we find our new tribe sheltered among the pines. But although Cruinn and our brethren have tried their best to settle their fears, the faces of the villagers remain awash with tears.

'And ...?' says Cruinn, expectantly. He is tending to Eithni, who, I am glad to see, is now awake and in good spirits.

'It was as we expected,' I say quietly. 'They are all gone.'

'And Father Melachlin?' says Feargus. 'And the others?'

The making of a frown is almost enough.

'The end was quick,' I offer.

'Do we dare return?' asks Cruinn.

'No,' I say. 'The sight of their butchered kin would be too much for these children to bear.'

'So where do we go now?' says Feargus. 'Do we return to the coast? Perhaps return to Hibernia? It might be safer there.'

'It might be safer, yes,' says Niamh. 'But I doubt that it is the correct path for us to take. Cruinn, do you know this area? Are there any other villages in close proximity? Villages that may likely accept these refugees?'

'There are always villages scattered about,' says Cruinn. 'And yes. If I am not mistaken, they will gladly accept these people. Especially the children. They are all

Picts, after all. Their loyalties stretch further than their own villages.'

'Then that must be our mission,' says Niamh. 'To see these people to safety and to warn others of the impending dangers that the Norsemen bring.'

'Are you willing,' I shout to our brethren, 'to join Brother Eamon and I in leading these people to safety? … Feargus?'

Feargus scratches his head before replying.

'What you say is true,' he says. 'A return to Hibernia may be the safest option, but this path is clearly the most Godly.'

'So then, my brethren?' I ask. 'Are we as one?'

To my surprise, my brothers respond with a resounding cheer.

'And you, Cruinn,' I say. 'What say you? Are you with us?'

'It seems there is no other way,' says Cruinn. 'I will stay with you, at least until these people are resettled. But I warn you. I have no desire to return to the life of a travelling monk.'

Nor do I, I think, and I reach to Niamh for a passionate embrace. I hear my brothers gasp, but I do not care. They will learn the truth of Brother Eamon soon enough. I take her hand and lead her into the gloom of the forest.

'Come,' I say. 'I believe there will be safety and freedom on the other side.'

ABOUT THE AUTHOR

Calder Garret is the author of *The Chatton Trilogy*, a series of hard-boiled crime novels, and *Kylie Teale Investigates*, a collection of cozy mystery short stories. Both *The Chatton Trilogy* and *Kylie Teale Investigates* explore small town life in the Australian outback and are available on Amazon.

f

Printed in Great Britain
by Amazon

87643729R00084